JADE GREEN

a ghost story

⇥ Books By Phyllis Reynolds Naylor ⇤

Shiloh
Shiloh Season
Saving Shiloh

The Agony of Alice
Alice in Rapture, Sort of
Reluctantly Alice
All but Alice
Alice in April
Alice In-Between
Alice the Brave
Alice in Lace
Outrageously Alice
Achingly Alice
Alice on the Outside
The Grooming of Alice

The Mad Gasser of Bessledorf Street
The Bodies in the Bessledorf Hotel
Bernie and the Bessledorf Ghost
The Face in the Bessledorf Funeral Parlor
The Bomb in the Bessledorf Bus Depot
The Treasure of Bessledorf Hill
Peril in the Bessledorf Parachute Factory

Witch's Sister
Witch Water
The Witch Herself

Walking Through the Dark
How I Came to be a Writer
How Lazy Can You Get?
Eddie, Incorporated

All Because I'm Older
Shadows on the Wall
Faces in the Water
Footprints at the Window
The Boy with the Helium Head
A String of Chances
The Solomon System
Night Cry
The Dark of the Tunnel
The Keeper
The Year of the Gopher
Beetles, Lightly Toasted
Maudie in the Middle
One of the Third Grade Thonkers
Send No Blessings
Josie's Troubles
The Fear Place
Ice
Being Danny's Dog
Danny's Desert Rats
Sang Spell
Walker's Crossing
Jade Green
The Grand Escape
The Healing of Texas Jake

PICTURE BOOKS
Ducks Disappearing
I Can't Take You Anywhere
Old Sadie and the Christmas Bear
Keeping a Christmas Secret
King of the Playground

JADE GREEN

a ghost story

PHYLLIS REYNOLDS
NAYLOR

ALADDIN PAPERBACKS
NEW YORK · LONDON · TORONTO · SYDNEY · SINGAPORE

First Aladdin Paperbacks edition June 2001

Aladdin Paperbacks
An imprint of Simon & Schuster
Children's Publishing Division
1230 Avenue of the Americas
New York, NY 10020

Also available in an Atheneum Books for Young Readers hardcover edition

The text for this book was set in Bembo.
Designed by Sammy Yuen Jr.

Printed and bound in the United States of America

10 9 8 7 6 5 4 3

The Library of Congress has cataloged the hardcover edition as follows:

Naylor, Phyllis Reynolds.
Jade green: a ghost story / by Phyllis Reynolds Naylor.
p.   cm.
Summary: While living with her uncle in a house haunted by the ghost of a
young woman, recently orphaned Judith Sparrow wonders if her one small
transgression causes mysterious happenings.
ISBN: 0-689-82005-4 (hc.)
  [1. Haunted houses—Fiction. 2. Ghosts—Fiction. 3. Orphans—Fiction. 4.
Uncles—Fiction.] I. Title
PZ7.N24Jad 2000 [Fic]—dc21 99-20740
ISBN: 0-689-82002-X (Aladdin pbk.)

For Jeanie, with love

One

WHEN THE carriage turned onto Stone Street, it was as though the house were watching. There were two gables with a window in each, the curtains slightly parted like cats' eyes, not quite closed, spying.

Earlier that day I had arrived by train in Charleston, and had at once been restless to move about after the tiresome journey from Ohio. Indeed, I felt constrained in my long gray skirt and jacket, a bonnet of gray and blue on my head. I was hungry as well, for in the first few hours I had eaten all the bread and cheese I had packed for the trip.

Even more, I longed for someone to talk to. As I have an adventurous spirit, I asked the driver, who met me at the station, if I could sit up front with him rather than in the carriage. There was still a considerable way to go before we reached the town of Whispers.

"An odd name for a town," I said to the man, a good-hearted soul with a red face and large ears, who helped me onto the driver's bench, where there was a much better view than any you could have in the carriage.

"They say it was named for the trees, Miss Sparrow," he answered, hauling himself up beside me with many a grunt and wheeze. "It's the sound they make when the wind blows through 'em—like old ladies they are, always whispering." And then, with a final look around to see that what little I owned in this world was secure on the rack, he gave a soft "Gee, up!" and the horse began its two-hour journey to the place where I would spend the rest of my life, God willing.

I was much gratified when the man drew from his coat pocket a cinnamon bun, and I accepted eagerly. "You're comin' to help out the cook, eh?" he said, leaning forward so that his elbows rested on his knees, all the better to stand the long ride, I suppose.

"Yes, sir," I answered, "and it's a good thing they'd have me, for not one other relative would take me in."

"You're orphaned, then?"

I nodded. "My father died four years ago September, and my mother died last month." I did not tell him that after my father's death she gave birth to a stillborn daughter, all of which grieved her so that she eventually died in a madhouse. "But now," I said more brightly, "I will live in South Carolina and be cousin and housekeeper both. Tell me about the house."

"Ah, Miss," he said. "That old place is . . ." He paused.

"Haunted?" I teased.

He startled. "It could use some cheer, and your uncle will be pleased to have you," the driver said quickly.

"I don't know about that," I told him. "It wasn't right away he agreed to take me in, and then only because there was no one else."

The driver gave me as kind a smile as I had ever seen. "He'll take one look at you and be glad he let you come," he said.

"And my cousin?" I asked. "It will be wonderful having a friend my own age to talk with."

"Why, Mister Charles is old enough to be your father. Near forty, I 'spect," the driver said.

"Forty!" I cried in dismay. "Surely not!"

"That he is, Miss. And he don't live with his father, neither. Takes some rooms in town, I believe. No birds of a feather, them two."

I slumped back against the seat, too disappointed to say more. How could it be that I was fifteen and Charles so old? True, I had never laid eyes on him except when I was so small I could not remember, living far from the home of my Southern relatives. But the more I thought about it, I realized that Uncle Geoffrey was twelve years my father's senior, and while he and his wife may have had their child early, my parents had me late.

"Well, never mind," I said at last, finishing the cinnamon bun. "I shall make them glad I have come and do my best."

"Of course you will," said the driver, and we passed the rest of the time discussing the climate, which, he said, I would find different from Ohio. The storms off the Carolina coast were legendary, he told me. But Emma Hastings, the cook, would make up for it, for she had a heart as warm as an oven, and big as the moon.

"Do you play the piano, Miss?" he asked. "They've a grand piano in the parlor."

"A little," I told him. Indeed, I had only eight years' schooling, which was quite enough, it was decided, for a girl of my station, though less than some of the boys I knew had acquired. But I could play the piano well enough to amuse myself and, at times, entertain others as well.

There was a carriage robe under the seat, and I wrapped it about me as we rode. I had hoped, when the train first arrived in Charleston, to find flowers near bloom but had been disappointed that spring had not yet come to this part of the country, either. The tips of the trees were a soft pink, but the land along the road to Whispers had a chilled gray look.

It was when we turned up Stone Street that I felt the first foreboding. The bare branches of the trees that lined our path seemed like slender fingers reaching out to ensnare me, and the trees themselves did not whisper so much as scrape and scratch as the carriage went by.

Then at the end of the street, the house—the large brown house with the two eyes—made me suddenly clutch at the driver's arm as if to say, *Turn back! Turn back!*

"It's all right, Miss," the driver said. "It's a big, dark house, but Emma Hastings is a good sort. She'll look out for you."

The long journey from Ohio had unnerved me, I

decided, for here I had a home, at least, and a forty-year-old cousin was better than no cousin at all. I had already been told that Uncle Geoffrey spoke little, so I did not expect encouragement or conversation there, but I resolved to be cheerful and obedient nonetheless.

Obedient except in one small thing, and my heart began to race as I remembered my obstinance. The solicitor had told me that there was a certain condition to living in my uncle's house: I could bring along whatever I liked except anything of the color green. This was strictly forbidden.

Such a strange demand, I'd thought. I had a green dress and some trinkets I would have to leave behind, yet for the offer of a roof over my head, I agreed to the terms.

As I packed for the journey, however, I decided that promise or no, there was one thing I would not—*could* not—leave behind: a photograph of my mother, which she had given to me in a frame of green silk. How I dared to disobey a man I had not even met, save when I was small—the only person who would give me shelter—now seemed a frightening thing indeed. Yet I yearned so for my mother that I had placed the photograph and frame at the bottom of my trunk, beneath my summer clothes, and there it rested as we neared my uncle's.

Thus, obedient to all his wishes but one, I alighted from the carriage, my eyes on the house, and opened the iron gate.

Two

THE DRIVER hesitated when we got to the front steps, setting my trunk down as though he would go no farther. As soon as I put one foot on the porch, however, the heavy oak door swung open, and I was immediately enveloped in the two round arms of Emma Hastings, the cook.

"Judith Sparrow, you are welcome here indeed!" she cried.

I would have replied in kind, but my head was pressed against her large bosom, crimping the rim of my bonnet. As soon as I righted myself, she led me into the hall, and the driver brought my bags and boxes. At Mrs. Hastings' instructions, he heaved and jockeyed my trunk up the stairs while I took off my bonnet and rearranged my dress. He seemed eager to leave, though, and as soon as he came down again and had been properly paid, I thanked him for his company and he went on his way.

Turning my attention to the interior of the house, I observed the high ceilings and the long flight of stairs leading to the floor above. The wainscoting and walls were of a deep brown, and the heavy velvet drapes at the windows a pale rose. On either side of the great hall were paintings of the Sparrow family, my uncle's side. Uncle Geoffrey and his deceased wife, both dressed in gray, were to the right, and my cousin Charles, their only son, on the left, in brown.

At that very moment there were footsteps on the stairs, and I looked up to see a man of sixty years coming down to meet me.

"She's here!" cried Mrs. Hastings. "And what she has brought, sir, would hardly fill a closet. She'll be no trouble at all."

Uncle Geoffrey gave only the faintest smile. If I had not been watching his mouth so closely, I might not even have recognized it as such, except that it so much resembled my late father's.

"And how was the journey?" he asked, shaking

my hand, but with no great enthusiasm, I noticed.

"I survived it well, but am very glad to be here, and thank you from the bottom of my heart for taking me in," I told him. "I intend to earn my keep, Uncle, and will do all I can to help Mrs. Hastings."

"I know she will," said the cook, squeezing my arm. While my uncle had thinning white hair and a pale complexion, Mrs. Hastings was pink-cheeked, her head topped with a mop of gray curls, putting my own long, straight hair to shame.

"We'll have dinner in an hour or so," she told me, picking up my small valise. "Let me show you your room and then we'll see you at table."

I picked up another travel bag, and Uncle Geoffrey followed with the rest.

What a welcome surprise that I should be given a bedroom on the second floor with the others. I had thought I might be lucky to have a room in the attic, but I was taken to a corner bedroom, with a four-poster bed and a chest of drawers, as well as writing desk and chair.

Mrs. Hastings showed me the closet where I should store my trunk, and pointed out the windows overlooking the garden below. There was a yellow quilt on my bed, a blue cushion on my chair, and I was most pleased with what I found.

When they left me to unpack my things, I

wondered, with each dress I hung in my closet, how long that dress would hang there, and whether or not this was to be my final destination, the only house to call home. Better than many girls had, to be sure.

Carefully I opened all the drawers in my dresser and gently placed inside them my linens and stockings and gloves. It was when I reached the bottom of my trunk that I saw my mother's picture in its green silk frame, and remembered once again how I had disobeyed the conditions for my coming. I knew only that the color green upset Uncle Geoffrey for some reason, and vowed therefore that he should never see it. What remained unseen could upset no one, I told myself. And so I kept it where it was, at the bottom of my trunk, and shoved the trunk far back in the closet.

"Well, Miss Sparrow," I said, looking at myself in the mirror—at my long brown hair and gray eyes, and a mouth a little too large for my face. "It seems you have a family now. And here is your room, all done up in yellow."

As I said the words, I let my eyes roam about the walls and floor and, turning, I saw that there was truly nothing green in sight. I went to the doorway and looked out into the hall, then over the banister to the floor below. All was brown and rose, gray and black.

No matter, I thought. Every family is odd in some way, and this shall be our peculiarity.

After I had changed my dress so as to be more presentable at dinner, I went downstairs and into the dining room where Uncle Geoffrey sat at the head of the table, waiting.

"I hope I'm not late," I said. "I was just admiring my room, Uncle."

"I trust you found it to your liking," he told me. And then, motioning to a chair to his left, he said, "You may sit there, Judith. Mrs. Hastings will sit across from you, and when Charles comes, he will sit at the other end. We will not wait for Charles, Emma."

"Very good, sir," she said from the doorway of the kitchen, and at once began ladling up the soup.

"I will see my cousin, then?" I asked pleasantly.

"He takes dinner with us most nights," my uncle replied.

I was pleased to know that he was coming, and that the cook was allowed to eat with us, for I would have found it awkward to converse with Uncle Geoffrey alone.

"How long have you lived here?" I asked Mrs. Hastings, wondering myself about the "Mrs." part.

"Since my Henry died some seventeen years ago," she said. "I was here when you visited as a wee babe, but of course you've no memory of that."

"She knows this house as well as I do. *Better* than I do, in fact," said my uncle.

We finished our soup and then the fish that Mrs. Hastings had poached. I was wondering that my cousin had not yet made his appearance when I heard the front door open, then close, and a somewhat portly man of forty years, a younger version of his father, came into the room with no apology for his tardiness and took his place at the table. Mrs. Hastings immediately rose to bring him both soup and fish.

As he tucked his napkin under his chin, Cousin Charles looked at me and said, "Well, I see our orphan girl has arrived, and I daresay she has chosen the best room for herself and eaten most of the fish."

My face grew warm, and I opened my mouth to protest, when Charles broke into laughter and said, "Only a joke, Judith. I hope you find your new home satisfactory."

"Yes, it's lovely," I said. "My room looks out on the garden, and I fancy I can see the sea beyond."

"Not quite," said Charles, spooning his soup into his mouth, "but it's only a short ride from here to the ocean, and when the windows are open in summer, you can sometimes hear the waves crashing against the shore."

"Oh, I will love living here, I know!" I said, delighted that I should make friends with the ocean with so little effort on my part.

Uncle Geoffrey said, "You were detained, Charles, I presume?"

"Yes, I was speaking to a man at the club who might have a position open as bookkeeper in his firm," Charles replied.

"That would seem a fitting job for you," said his father.

"Fitting, perhaps, but boring. Nonetheless, I'll think about it," Charles answered.

"A bird in hand . . .," offered Mrs. Hastings.

"Oh, Emma, you would delight in seeing me take any job at all, just so I would not stop by here so often," Charles said amiably.

"It's only that I think you should find your current unemployment even more boring, sir," she said. And then, reflecting perhaps that she had said enough, she got up to serve the veal, and I found myself seated between father and son, knowing that neither of them had especially wanted me.

"If you will instruct me, Uncle, as to my duties here, I would like to begin as soon as possible," I said, looking directly at Uncle Geoffrey. His skin hung loosely about the jaw and chin, whereas Charles had several chins, and a light red beard growing in a fringe around the edge of his face.

"I'll leave that to Mrs. Hastings," Uncle Geoffrey said. "She will find plenty for you to do, and what you do in your spare time is your business. I have my duties, Charles has his, so please do not expect us to entertain you. We have no desire to turn you into a servant, however, and you may come and go as you please, as long as Mrs. Hastings is satisfied."

I could not believe I should be treated so well, and thanked him not once, but several times over.

After the veal there was cheese and wine, and though the dinner was far better than any I had eaten before, something seemed to be missing. I could not decide what it was. Then, as the pecan tarts were served, half drowned in whipped cream, I realized that there was nothing green on the table: no beans or peas or spinach. Even in winter, my mother had managed to serve green beans that she had put up in the summer. Well, I decided, the residents here look healthy enough, and I vowed I would not worry about it further.

I stayed in the kitchen later with Mrs. Hastings until every fork and plate had been washed and put away. Then, long since exhausted, I bid her good night, went upstairs to my room, and sat myself down, relieved to be alone. I had scarcely the energy to take off my dress and petticoats. Finally, drawing my gown over my head, I slipped off my stockings, blew out the candle, and settled down beneath the covers.

So fast was I falling asleep that I scarcely heard it at first—a faint scratching sound from my closet. My eyes opened a little, then closed.

The sound came again. This time I rose up on one elbow and listened. It was part scratching, part gnawing or clawing, as though something was trapped within the wall or behind the baseboard—a light, gentle noise that did not seem urgent enough to rouse me.

"So we have mice," I said aloud, and gave myself over to sleep.

Three

I WOKE THE next morning scarcely knowing where I was. But when I saw the sun shining full in the window, turning the yellow curtains white with its brilliance, I jumped out of bed, washed, and dressed, afraid that my uncle would think me the laziest creature alive.

As I brushed my hair, I happened to look out the window to see Mrs. Hastings in the garden below, bending over some plants that were just showing themselves above ground. I clattered eagerly downstairs and out the back door.

"I'm sorry I slept so long," I apologized.

"Is there anything I can do to help?"

Mrs. Hastings pushed back her gray curls and turned to smile at me. "Come look," she said. "My peas are shooting up already."

"But . . . but, they're green!" I said, which was all too obvious. "I thought—"

"Ah, I cook them in a pot outdoors, and we eat them in the garden," the cook said, pointing to a wrought-iron table and chairs under the beech tree. "In summer, this is where we have our salads." And then, changing the subject, she took my arm and led me back to the house, where she made a most splendid breakfast.

"What are my duties here?" I asked as I took more cream for my tea. "Uncle said I was to ask you."

"Keep an old woman company, mostly," she answered. "We do have a gardener who helps out now and then, but you can weed when you like. Help out in the kitchen when needed. Tidy up the rooms. In truth, my dear, there's not all that much for you to do, but if you wish, Helene's Hat Shoppe could use a ribbon clerk, and I would be glad to recommend you."

I could hardly contain my delight, for I liked the idea that I might earn money of my own. "Oh, yes!" I told her.

"We want you to be happy here, my girl," Mrs.

Hastings continued. "If anything upsets you, you must let me know." This last was spoken with such gravity that I wondered what she could mean.

"What could possibly upset me?" I asked. "You have all been so kind."

Mrs. Hastings busied herself at the stove. "Just . . . just anything at all. Things you might hear . . . or notice. . . ."

"Well," I said. "There is one thing . . ."

She turned and looked at me in alarm. "What?" she asked.

"I think there are mice in my closet," I told her.

At that she threw back her head and broke into laughter, looking much relieved. "Is that all? I'll get you a trap, and we'll have done with those mice. I'll not have the nasty things chewing on your slippers. The least we can do is keep them down here in the kitchen where they belong." And then she laughed again most merrily, and I too joined in.

That afternoon I was up to my elbows in flour, for Mrs. Hastings was teaching me to make chicken pie. We had brought up potatoes and onions from the root cellar beneath the kitchen, and now we were working the crust.

"Keep a light touch, my girl," she instructed, "but the shortening and flour must be cut together fine, like so."

I had just rubbed one arm against my nose when suddenly there was a knock at the back door, and in walked a tall boy with hair as blond as ever I saw. He had a broad back, and carried a large bag of flour over one shoulder.

"Hello, Zeke," said Mrs. Hastings. "Put it down, my man, but not on the girl's piecrust."

It was too late. Zeke squatted down beside me and, in his haste to get the heavy bag off his shoulder and onto the edge of the table, he misjudged the distance, and the bag rolled over onto my breadboard.

"Now there's a clumsy oaf if ever I saw one!" Mrs. Hastings cried, but she was chuckling all the while, and when Zeke looked at me, with flour on my face, he laughed too, and soon we were all at it.

"Zeke Carey is the miller's son, and our delivery-man as well," the cook explained. "If there's anything you need, he can get it for you."

"And you must be Judith, all the way from the cold North," Zeke said in amusement.

"Well, Ohio is not exactly the Arctic Circle," I said, wanting him to see that I knew my geography, at least. "But I'm very glad to be here."

"And *we* are very glad to have you too," he told me. The way he said the word "we" made my cheeks redden, but Mrs. Hastings was smiling, and I half believed she'd put him up to it.

He grinned as he reached around her and helped himself to a biscuit left over from breakfast. "So what do you do when you're not dusting yourself with flour?" he asked me.

"I just got here yesterday," I said.

"She'll be busy enough. Don't you go putting ideas in her head," Mrs. Hastings warned him.

But Zeke looked straight into my eyes. "When it grows warm, you'll go to the shore with me," he said. "You'll like that—our ocean."

He did not ask, he told me, and I could tell by the way Mrs. Hastings had to shoo him out of the kitchen with her apron, as though he were a pestering goose, that here was a young man who was not afraid to speak his mind.

In the late afternoon I did my dusting, and was glad enough to do it, for it gave me an excuse to see every room. There was the dining room, with its long table and sideboard, each chair with an acorn carved on its back; the living room, with its stained-glass panels above each window, its massive fireplace, the velvet-covered chairs and rose sofa, and the grand piano as black and shiny as coal. With great pleasure I dusted each key, sounding it softly, and knew that, undistinguished player that I was, I would play it even so. Then there was my uncle Geoffrey's study, piled high with books and papers, and the sunroom with the wicker furniture.

When I had finished the first floor, I went up to second, where there were five bedrooms and the water closet. Mrs. Hastings and I had the two bedrooms at the back of the house while Uncle Geoffrey had one of the corner bedrooms facing the front. The other belonged to Charles, which was kept for him even though he stayed in town. The fifth bedroom, the smallest, was located just at the top of the stairs, and seemed to be used for storage. There were fishing rods and old lamps, and, on the spare bed, a pile of quilts and hatboxes.

In each of the bedrooms, save that one and Charles's, I made the beds, plumped the pillows, and dusted the dressers. I was curious about the spare bedroom, however. What intrigued me was that, in addition to the closet, there was still another door. When I opened it, I saw narrow stairs leading upward.

"I would not go up there," a voice said.

I wheeled about to see Cousin Charles watching me from the hallway. It startled me, for I had not known he was in the house.

"The attic is full of cobwebs and dust—you'd get your dress dirty." He smiled, then, and his eyes traveled the length of my dress.

"I . . . I was not planning to go up," I said. "I was checking to see if there was something in need of dusting."

"Certainly nothing up there," he told me, and went on down to the kitchen.

In the next few days, I discovered that one did not know when Cousin Charles was around and when he was not. I might see him walking briskly down the sidewalk and out the iron gate, hat on head and cane in hand as though heading for an important engagement, and an hour later he might be lying on the divan in the sunroom, reading the newspaper. Or he would say he was taking a coach into town, yet not long after, I would hear his footsteps on the stairs. Mrs. Hastings told me he was not at all like Uncle Geoffrey, who would leave for work at the same time every morning, Sundays excepted, and arrive home for dinner at the same time every evening. For a man who did not live here, Charles was very much in evidence.

"What does Charles do?" I asked Mrs. Hastings one afternoon as I helped her peel the onions for stew. "Does he work?"

"One is never too sure of Charles," Mrs. Hastings answered. "Now and then he takes employment. I don't know just where."

.   .   .

A few days later, she gave me a mousetrap and some cheese.

"Set this in your closet, Judith, and in a few nights' time, I imagine, you shall have the mice that are pestering you," she said.

I thanked her and, that night before I blew out my candle, put the cheese in the trap and set it on my closet floor. I heard nothing more that night or the night after, but the third night, there came that same scratching sound as before, but louder now, more insistent, a determined clawing as though some small animal *would* make it through the wall of my closet, like it or no.

Sitting up, I swung my legs over the side of the bed and lit my candle. There was a light *thunk* from the closet, and the scratching stopped. I crept to the closet door and opened it slowly. It creaked, in need of a good oiling.

Slowly, slowly, I pushed my clothes to one side so as to see the back of that tiny room, holding the candle out in front of me. There was the mousetrap still set, the cheese untouched. Nothing was nibbled, nothing chewed. The air seemed suddenly colder, though, and I wrapped one arm about me, goose pimples rising on my flesh. What caught my eye, however, was my trunk. I took a step forward and held the candle closer. The lid had been closed when I'd put it away, I was sure of it, but now it had been raised a few inches and rested slightly askew on its frame.

Four

KNEELING ON the floor of the closet, the candle casting an eerie light among the shadows, I felt most apprehensive and my flesh grew colder still. It appeared as though someone had been searching my possessions and had carelessly left the lid of my trunk ajar.

What if my uncle had found my mother's picture in its green silken frame? Would I then, for my disobedience, be put out into the street with no one in this world to protect me?

With shaking hands, I set the candle on the floor and crawled toward the trunk at the back.

Whack!

With a cry, I flung myself around as something grabbed at my foot. Then my breath gave way in relief, for I saw that I had foolishly set off the mousetrap and caught my toe in it. Wincing with pain, I released the trap and turned my attention once again to the lid of the trunk.

Cautiously I raised it, afraid even to peer inside. But the framed picture was right where I had left it, beneath my summer dresses. Nothing seemed amiss except that the trunk lid had been opened slightly.

Well, thought I, either I left the lid ajar when I put the trunk away, or Mrs. Hastings came to see that I was settled, and gave it a quick inspection. I would know soon enough at breakfast the next day.

And so, still worried about my future in my new household, I reset the mousetrap, blew out my candle, and crawled back under the covers, glad that my small scream had awakened no one. It was some time, however, before I slept.

When I did open my eyes again, it was morning, and rain was beating against the window. I got out of bed and put on my second-best dress, my black stockings, and my wool shawl, for this was the day Mrs. Hastings was accompanying me to Helene's Hat Shoppe, where I would be interviewed for a job. I entered the kitchen somewhat nervously, but our cook was her usual cheerful self.

"Now *that's* a nice frock!" she exclaimed, looking over my red and white dress with the black ribbon around the collar and hem. "You'll make a good impression on Helene, my girl. Here. I've warmed some biscuits for you."

Since I rarely got up the same time as my uncle, I liked having breakfast in the kitchen with Mrs. Hastings.

"Any luck with those mice?" she asked.

"Not yet," I answered truthfully.

"Well, they're wary at first, but one of these days one will venture into that trap, you watch," she said.

At that moment we heard Cousin Charles enter the front door. He came on out to the kitchen, looking surprised to see me dressed as I was, and eyed my frock with approval. "You ladies appear to be going somewhere," he said, noting that Mrs. Hastings wore a dress without apron. He took a cup from the cupboard that she might pour him some coffee, which she did at once.

"We're going to Helene's Hat Shoppe, where I am to be interviewed for a job!" I told him excitedly.

I had expected he would welcome the opportunity for me to have an income of my own, but I could see from the set of his mouth that the news did not particularly please him.

"Helene's Gossip Shoppe, I'd call it," said he. "You'll hear more stories there than there are in a book of fables."

"Our Judith has a fine head on her shoulders. I daresay she will be able to tell truth from gossip," said Mrs. Hastings. "It will do her good to be out making friends. Now if you will take your coffee into the parlor and out of my way, Charles, I will get this bread to rising before we leave."

Charles left the kitchen grumbling, and Mrs. Hastings shook her head as she worked. "Sometimes a person has to speak her mind," she said. "Besides, it's not him pays my wages, it's Mr. Sparrow. Now! Go get your bonnet, my girl, and we'll be off."

By the time we started out, the rain of that morning had stopped, and though we had to watch for puddles, I took great pleasure in walking the half mile to Helene's Hat Shoppe. The whispering trees that lined the streets had now begun to take on a faint green hue, the newest of leaves unfolding, and I was happy that Mrs. Hastings had made no mention of my trunk; I began to suspect I had not closed the lid as I'd thought.

The hat shop was a little nook in a row of shops

along King Street. It had a pink door, pink shutters, and a little bell that dinged as soon as one entered. Helene Harper was a tall, thin woman with reddish-brown hair which, if I may venture a guess, was the result of dye, for her face was quite wrinkled. Nonetheless, I excused her this deception, for she was most gracious and dressed so elegantly, I could not help but be thrilled that I might be employed by such a woman of fashion.

"This is our Judith," Mrs. Hastings said proudly.

"How do you do?" asked Helene, and her smile was as fine as her dress. We talked briefly about what had brought me to Whispers, and I could tell that all the time I was answering her questions, she was observing my manner of speech and the posture with which I sat, and my fingernails, which I'd scrubbed and trimmed that very morning. When I had finally answered her questions, she said to Mrs. Hastings, "I think she will do very well here, Emma. We'll let her sample the work today, and if it's to her liking, she shall begin at full salary next week."

How glad I was! Mrs. Hastings hugged me and went back home, and I was introduced to the other girl in the shop, a young woman two years my senior by the name of Violet Morrison.

"When a woman comes in for a new bonnet,"

Helene explained, "I help her find a style that will fit her face, and we decide how it should be trimmed. Then Violet, here, will put the creation together. Your job, Judith, is to keep the cupboard stocked with lace and ribbon, and to cut the amounts we need for each hat, measuring just so. Violet will teach you the art of hatmaking so that in time, if you are observant, you may work up to hatmaking yourself, with an accompanying raise in wages. But for now," she added, "you and Violet shall get acquainted, and I will let her show you how we cut and measure."

The small bell on the front door jingled, and she went over to admit a large woman in a lavender coat. I went into the back room with Violet, who had hair far darker than mine, large brown eyes, and a figure slightly on the plump side.

"I am *so* glad you've come!" she said. "I begged and begged Helene to take you on, sight unseen, for truly I get bored stitching back here by myself all day, especially when Helene is with customers. Are you sure your uncle will let you work?"

"Oh, yes," I answered. "He has already said I am free to come and go as I like."

"Aye, that's what he told the other girl, and look what happened to her!" said Violet darkly, pulling out a stool that she might stand on it to show me the bolts

31

of netting and the spools of ribbon on a shelf above the cutting table.

I took off my bonnet and laid it on a chair. "What other girl?" I asked.

"The girl who lived there before you. Jade Green. Didn't they tell you?"

"Why, no!" I said. "I've heard of no other girl."

"Ah! Then I've put my foot in it!" Violet exclaimed, clapping one hand over her mouth.

"No, please!" I said. "If I'm to live there, I need to know. Did she displease my uncle?"

Violet studied me uncertainly, but made no answer.

"Violet, you *must* tell me!" I begged. "Where is she now? Did he turn her out?"

She looked around anxiously, as though afraid someone might be listening. "He didn't turn her out, Judith, and what went on in that house, I really can't say. But the girl was Jade Green, and she's been dead for three years."

Five

A WEAKNESS OVERCAME me, and I could hardly catch my breath.

"Dead?" I cried. "There has not been mention of her name since I entered the house! I have heard not a word of it since I came to Whispers!"

"Nor will you, I imagine," said Violet, her voice low. "Your uncle would like never to hear of it again, I'm sure, for what a dreadful shock to have someone die in his very own home!"

"Had she taken an illness?"

"Took her own *life,*" said Violet, retrieving a bolt

of blue veiling from the shelf above and stepping off the stool again.

I gasped and put one hand to my throat. "But who was she? Why was she living in Uncle Geoffrey's house?"

"Because he's a Christian man, and the girl was penniless, with nowhere to go. The reverend at the church asked about, if any would take her in, and at last she found a home where you are now."

"Did you know her?"

"Not well. She worked over at the butcher shop, but I saw her now and then at the Bib and Bottle. She was . . ."

Helene's tall figure appeared in the doorway. "Violet!" she said sternly. "I will not have gossip in my shop. The matter of Miss Green is not to be spoken of here again. Is that understood?"

"Yes, ma'am," said Violet, her cheeks turning pink as she quickly spread the veiling out on the counter.

"I hope you young women will be friends, but please keep those wretched stories out of my hearing," Helene added.

"We will, ma'am," Violet replied quickly.

When Helene had gone back into the next room, Violet and I exchanged looks as we bent over our task.

"I'll save the rest till we're *out* of the shop then," said Violet mischievously. I could not help but smile and feel that I had found a lively friend.

There was much to learn about hats, and I came away that day, my head spinning with sizes, shapes, brims, crowns—so much so that my temples throbbed. But the walk home in the spring air was much to my liking.

As soon as I turned onto Stone Street, however, it was as though the house with the gables were grinning at me, that it knew far more than I had discovered thus far. Once again I felt the same foreboding, and decided that the best course was to approach Mrs. Hastings directly about the matter. For although I could imagine my uncle taking in a hapless young woman without a penny to her name and giving her shelter, just as he had done for me, I could not understand why a then so fortunate a creature would take her own life.

As soon as I was seated in the kitchen with Mrs. Hastings over a cup of tea, my bonnet in my lap, I said, "Mrs. Hastings, there's something disturbing me deeply, and I don't know who else to ask except you."

I had expected the cook to assure me that she would put my fears, whatever they may be, to rest. I could see, however, that she seemed almost to stop breathing, and I began to think that she very much wished I would not ask my question at all. Nonetheless, what had been started must be carried through, I told myself.

"Why is it that no one has told me that a girl named Jade Green lived in this house and that she died by her own hand?"

Mrs. Hastings blanched as white as an onion, and her lips worked awkwardly before she spoke: "My dear, there was indeed a young woman whom your uncle befriended at the request of the clergy, and she died here some three years ago. I thought it might frighten you to learn of this, coming as you did to a strange house in a faraway town with not a soul you could call friend. I decided that after you felt more settled here, I could tell you about Jade Green."

"Well," I said, "you are a dear to have such regard for my feelings, but I am now settled and ready to listen." I pushed my teacup away and gave her my full attention.

Mrs. Hastings continued to stir her own tea long after she had put in the sugar and milk.

"She was quite a young thing when she came to us, not more than twelve and, if I may speak plainly, little more than a street urchin. She had never known her father, and her mother was of that profession few women care to mention, so Jade had been left to herself more often than not. She had spent her days on the street begging or stealing, for she did not much care for school, and the school, in truth, did not care for her at all.

"When the reverend came calling on Mr. Sparrow to see if he might take her in—ours being a large house, well-situated in the heart of town and convenient to a young girl's needs—I spoke in her favor, for Mr. Hastings and I had long been childless. It seemed a blessing that this house—with Mrs. Sparrow since deceased—should have a young occupant again. And so your uncle agreed."

At this point Mrs. Hastings pulled a handkerchief from her sleeve and held it ready, as her eyes began to glisten.

"Oh, how I made ready for that girl!" she said. "I had been told that green was her favorite color, so I made an outfit just for her—green bonnet, green dress, a little green jacket to go over it all—and she was given the room at the top of the stairs, the small one, as the room you are in now was reserved for company."

Here Mrs. Hastings began to swallow and dab at her eyes, and I almost wished I had not asked my question at all. Still, I had to know. So I waited.

"Well, she was a handful, let me tell you. So used to sleeping in the gutter, she was, that for the first week I could not persuade her to lie in bed. It was only with the greatest difficulty that she learned to live as civilized people do, that she would put on stockings and speak with a civil tongue. But time and kindness won her over, and our little Jade slowly came to appreciate our ways.

"She could not be induced to return to school, however, by now being so far behind others her age. But she proved most proficient with her hands, and at last took a job in the butcher shop, where she received a steady wage. It was said she could bone a chicken in half the time it took the men, her fingers being small and nimble."

Mrs. Hastings stopped and sipped her tea, smiling a little at her memories. "What it was she brought to this house, it's hard to say. But where Mr. Sparrow was all stiffness and propriety, Jade Green was lighthearted and careless. Where Mr. Sparrow rarely smiled, Jade was a little prankster at times, and delighted in making him laugh. If the day dawned dark, or there was a storm at sea, it was Jade Green who became our sun, and before long Mr. Sparrow began asking for her as soon as he came in of an evening. 'Is Jade about?' he would say, and sometimes just knowing she was in the house or out in the garden was enough for him. He would settle himself down in his chair, assured that she would have a lively tale to tell him at dinner."

Here Mrs. Hastings's lower lip began to tremble. "Mr. Sparrow himself was as fond of her as if she were his own daughter, for he had no daughters of his own, you know. He read to her of an evening, and taught her to play simple tunes on the piano. Oftentimes, when she saw that he was tired, she would sit down in the parlor and make him a melody, and how his eyes would light up."

Suddenly the cook broke down altogether and began to sob. "We thought she ... she was happy here. We thought she ... felt at home. And then, there came the awful day that I found her body. . . ." Mrs. Hastings got up and stood at the window, shoulders shaking, until she could compose herself.

"Oh, dear Mrs. Hastings, I didn't wish to cause you such grief!" I cried.

But finally she continued: "The coroner said you can never tell about those people—it's in their makeup, these violent urges, these 'strange unaccountables,' he calls them. But from that time on, Mr. Sparrow declared that the color green would no longer be allowed in the house. And so, child, it is banished forever, and we never speak the girl's name in his presence."

I sat in silence, not knowing what else to do. Finally, as Mrs. Hastings turned from the window, I said, "I am so sorry, and hope that my stay here will help, in some small way, to ease the pain you have suffered."

"Indeed it has already," said Mrs. Hastings.

"But still," I continued, knowing that if I was never to speak of Jade again, I should do so now or forever after keep still, "the story you have told me is the same as that told me by Violet Morrison at the hat shop. Yet Cousin Charles suggested that what I should hear spoken there would be nothing but gossip, and Helene Harper herself, upon hearing our talk, declared it so. If this is truth, Mrs. Hastings, then what is the gossip that I should disregard?"

Once again I saw the cook's face stiffen, and she thrust her handkerchief back up her sleeve. "All you have heard thus far is true, Judith, but anything beyond this, I daresay, will be gossip."

And with that, she got out her broom and dustbin and began sweeping with such vigor that I knew that not only should I not ask any more questions of her, but that I should vacate the kitchen as well.

I went outside and walked through the garden, where the old gardener, bent and nearly deaf, was pruning a bush. I could scarcely sort out all the questions in my head. When I had arrived in Whispers, I'd felt sincerely that Mrs. Hastings, if anyone, was my friend, and that I could trust her with my life. But I knew as surely as I knew my own name that there was more to the story than this. And when I looked next at the house, I saw her studying me from behind the curtain and Cousin Charles watching from a window above.

Six

WHAT WAS I to do, and whom was I to trust? I could think of nothing but to go back in the house, for I had nowhere else to live.

Walking into the parlor, I looked about for something to distract me, that I should be in a better frame of mind when it was time for dinner. I sat down at the piano and played a piece my mother had taught me, "The Shepherd's Song," surprised at how clumsy my fingers were, not having touched piano keys for the past several years.

There was a book of songs on the piano, and I leafed through it, looking for one that did not tax my skill. I came upon a piece called "Springfield Mountain," but it was the words that caught my eye:

On Springfield Mountain there did dwell
A lovely youth I knowed him well.

This lovely youth one day did go
Down to the meadow for to mow.

He scarce had mowed quite round the field
When a cruel serpent bit his heel.

They took him home to Molly dear
Which made him feel so very queer.

Now Molly had two ruby lips
With which the poison she did sip.

Now Molly had a rotting tooth,
And so the poison killed them both.

Each verse was followed by the chorus, thus:

Too roo de nay, too roo de noo
Too roo de nay, too roo de noo.

What a strange song! I thought. Yet the tune was a simple one, repeated over and over, and one for which my fingers were well-suited, and so I began to play.

At once a voice behind me boomed: "Please stop!"

It startled me so that my hands slipped off the piano keys and into my lap. I turned around to see Uncle Geoffrey in the doorway, his face greatly agitated.

I didn't know what to say and finally blurted out, "I'm sorry, Uncle. I didn't think my playing would bother you, though I know how dreadfully I do it."

He looked flustered then. "You're welcome to play the piano; it's just that particular song. I don't care for it."

"As you wish," I said. I turned to the music book again and found another, "Evening Star," and played it through without incident. And then we were called to dinner.

Uncle Geoffrey was trying hard, I could tell, to make amends for so sorely frightening me in the parlor. As Mrs. Hastings served the roast duck, he said, "I understand that today was your first day in the hat shop, Niece. I hope that you found the work pleasant enough."

"I did indeed," I replied, "and as I learn the trade, there will be an increase in wages. So I'm quite content, and wish only not to shirk my duties here."

"Now don't you worry about that, my girl," Mrs.

Hastings put in. "The work around here will wait. The dust won't be going anywhere soon, and you can use the mop on a Tuesday as well as a Monday. A young girl like you shouldn't be shut up in a house all week, anyway."

"True enough," said Uncle Geoffrey. And then, to his son he asked, "And how did your day fare, Charles?"

"I was a bit late in rising, so I didn't go out until ten, but I did make a tour of the new town hall, Father, and find the architecture quite as grand as they said it would be."

Uncle Geoffrey sipped his wine and, putting down his glass, asked, "And did you, by chance, visit any of the offices there and ask what opportunities there might be for your employment?"

"Like a common beggar?" Charles asked irritably, drawing himself up straight. "Upon my word, Father, if there is a job suitable for my talents, I daresay *they* will come to *me*."

"They can hardly come to you if they don't know what your particular talents might be, and I am hard-pressed myself to describe them," his father said with displeasure.

This was as close to an argument as I had heard, and I kept my eyes on my plate, quickly helping myself to the turnips that Mrs. Hastings had handed me. But when dinner was over, and together Mrs.

Hastings and I were clearing up the dishes, there was an argument of such volume between Uncle Geoffrey and Cousin Charles in the parlor that even if we had covered our ears, we still should have heard every word. Just the clink of the brandy glass upon the tray told us how annoyed Uncle was when he set it down.

". . . whittling away your time!" he boomed. "At the grand age of forty, Charles, you have little to show for it. How am I to leave my estate to you when you have held no job worth mentioning to prove you can manage it?"

"And how am I to manage when I've little to practice on? If you refuse me more income, Father, there is nothing to invest, nothing to manage," countered Charles.

"And why must it be *my* property upon which you try your talents?" exploded his father. "Why haven't you made any effort to earn your own fortune? Then, when I see you can handle that, I will have no hesitation in leaving the estate in your name."

Mrs. Hastings and I looked at each other in the kitchen, embarrassed that we were overhearing such a personal conversation as this, yet every word came through the doorway as clearly as though spoken in our presence.

"They do go at it now and then," she said to me, pursing her lips. "Spoiled, he is, that Charles. Mrs.

Sparrow, she's the one who did it. Kept him here in the house waiting on her hand and foot—never asked anything of him but to take her about wherever she would go. After she died, Charles began doing all the things he couldn't do before."

"And now?" I said.

"Now that it's just Charles and his father, things are being said that should have been spoken years ago." She sighed. "But who am I? The cook, that's all. And so I hold my tongue." She smiled a little, and added, "Most of the time, anyway."

"Would you have me take on work beneath my station, like any poor beggar on the street, Father?" came Charles's voice once more.

"Never be ashamed of honest work, Charles. I would rather be shamed for idleness, as that."

"Well, just remember this," Cousin Charles replied, "I am your only living offspring. Don't be overly generous with others in your will."

"That's us," whispered Mrs. Hastings as we plunged our arms in the soapy water there in the sink. "You and me. So afraid is Charles that we might be left a copper penny or two that I think he would see us to the station himself if ever we were to leave Whispers."

"It's terrible having to live somewhere you're not wanted," I murmured.

"Oh, my girl, *I* want you here, and so does your uncle Geoffrey. Now don't you worry about Charles. His bark is worse than his bite."

"I'm afraid I displeased my uncle, though, by playing a song I found in the music book," I told her.

This time Mrs. Hastings did not look at me when she replied. "That was a song played often by Jade Green when she was here. He does not want to be reminded, that's all."

When the pots and pans had been put away, I went up to my room to read awhile before bedtime. As I was sitting by my window, turning the pages, I detected a soft scurrying sound from inside my closet.

"They're back," I said, listening for the sound of the mousetrap to spring. It did not snap, however, and after a minute or so, the scurrying stopped.

"I shall catch those mice yet!" I whispered, but was distracted just then by a shadow outside my open door. It did not move, but I could tell from where it lay that someone stood just around the doorway.

Putting down my book, I walked swiftly across the rug and came face-to-face with Charles in the hallway.

"I suppose," said he, "that you and Mrs. Hastings had your ears glued to the study door."

So shocked I was at his words that I scarce realized he had grabbed hold of my wrist.

"I assure you, sir, I was n-not listening intentionally," I stammered. "All I heard came to me in the kitchen unbidden." I tried, then, to pull away, cradling my hands against my chest.

A smile played about his lips, but his eyes never softened. "My father and I do argue from time to time," he said, "but it is nothing that involves you." He released my hand but, in withdrawing his own, let one finger slide down the buttons of my bodice. "Our affairs do not concern you in the least."

He turned then, and went swiftly back down the stairs.

Seven

I WAS GLAD that Charles lived in town, but I resolved then and there that whenever I was in my room, I should close the door, and did so at once. Then I retired for the evening, but sleep came fitfully. Turning first this way, then that, I rose once to open my window wider so as to let in the breeze, and finally dozed off into a restless slumber. I don't know what I dreamed, except that I wakened sometime in the night to the sound of a creaking door.

My eyes opened wide, and I lay there, one hand on my pounding heart. *Charles?* The door creaked again.

"Who is it?" I called.

There was no reply.

I reached for my candle, struck a match, and lit it. The room was empty. The door to the hallway was closed as I had left it, but the door to my closet was open several inches wide.

I lay there clutching the bedsheet to my chin in terror, for I was sure I had closed it, especially with mice nesting as they were inside. I did not blow out the candle, but let it burn the rest of the night, and what sleep there was seemed no sleep at all.

The next morning, with the sun shining full on my curtains, I concluded that perhaps I had not closed the closet door as I had thought and that the breeze coming in the window had blown the door to and fro.

Obviously, the nightmares I had experienced when my father died, then my mother, were revisiting themselves upon me. There were times I was seized with the terror that what had happened to my parents might also happen to me. The slightest sickness would bring with it thoughts of dying, and such morbid thoughts, in turn, made me fear my mother's madness. Work was the only solution, and since I would not begin at the hat shop until the following week, I went downstairs and announced to Mrs. Hastings that I would like more vigorous work to aid in my sleep, and she cheerfully complied. Fastening a towel around the bristles of a broom, she instructed me to go through the entire house sweeping down cobwebs from the ceilings.

"If that doesn't tire you, my girl, you can scrub both front and back porches," she laughed, "but I'll wager you'll scarcely hit the sheets tonight before you're asleep."

I set to work at once, sweeping the broom high overhead, running it along the moldings, traveling down the corners and around the gas lamps on the walls. I vowed never to go in Cousin Charles's room until I was certain he was out of the house, but when Mrs. Hastings confided that he had gone to the race-track, I cleaned the cobwebs from his ceiling also. Being thorough in my work, I did his closet too and could not help but be impressed at the number and variety of suits I found hanging there, even though he lived in town—clothes of the best cut and cloth. In short, he owned so much, he could not even keep them all at one place.

"How he lives and what he owns is no business of mine," I reminded myself, and moved on down the hall to the spare bedroom next to the water closet.

I knew when I entered it this time that I would not be so easily dissuaded from investigating the stairs to the attic. Mrs. Hastings had told me to tackle the cobwebs, but she did not tell me where to stop. So I took this as permission—instruction, even—to sweep down the cobwebs in the attic as well. I swept about the walls of the small bedroom with my broom, and when I had seen to that task, turned my attention to the door on one side, opening it slowly, revealing the narrow staircase.

Even though it was midmorning, the passageway was dark, so I got the candle from my room and, holding it in one hand, the broom in the other, I ascended the stairs a step at a time, my lips parted to let out my breath, so rapid had my breathing become.

The light from the candle cast huge shadows upon the slanted attic ceiling, and indeed, there was little space to walk, for the floor was so filled with boxes, trunks, and furniture that I could take only a few steps this way, then that. The air was heavy with the smell of dust, old cloth, and paper, and the curtains I had seen at the gable windows from out on the street proved to be yellowed, threadbare things, scarcely more than cobwebs themselves. Up here, the two gable windows struck me as even more fearsome, for they seemed to be eyes looking inward, studying my every move. I held the candle at arm's length to light the far corners, and satisfied myself that there was nothing out of the ordinary that could not be found in any attic.

Nothing moved save the shadows, and those only because my hand was trembling. And finally, much relieved, I forgot the cobwebs entirely and started down again.

Halfway from the bottom, my heart leaped against the wall of my chest, for there was a large, dark shadow on the remaining steps. I stood motionless, fearing that someone might be standing just outside the attic door. But as my breathing returned and I stepped cautiously upon one of the darkened steps and examined it more closely, I saw that it was not a shadow at all but a dark stain embedded in the wood.

Holding the candle over the deep mahogany stain, the pounding of my heart told me what my brain at first refused—that it was the color of blood. I had not thought it was there when I ascended the stairs, yet here it was, as sure as the slipper on my foot, and I wondered if my mind were turning against me.

I sucked in my breath and leaned against the wall, trying to conquer my terror. Yes, it was blood most certainly. Here was where the deed was done, I knew it now. I tried to imagine a girl like Jade Green hiding on the attic stairs and taking her life. What could have driven her to it—a girl as spunky and full of life as she had been, according to the cook?

I went swiftly on down, and when at last I was in the room below, I closed the attic door behind me and sat on the edge of the spare bed until finally my pulse slowed. The better I knew the house, I was certain, the less I would fear it, no matter what its tales, and the better I would sleep at night. But the blood on the staircase disturbed me greatly.

Nonetheless, I worked so hard all day that I slept very well that evening, and the next and the next. When I woke the morning of my first full day in Helene's Hat Shoppe, it was as though summer had come overnight to Whispers. Leaves that had been only tight little curls before had now unfolded, and a green world was appearing beyond my bedroom windows.

"Oh, Mrs. Hastings!" I cried, entering the kitchen. "It's a beautiful day!"

"Indeed it is!" she replied. "Your uncle took his coffee in the garden this morning before going to work, and I have biscuits and jam waiting for you too under the beech tree."

In truth, I had been so eager to get to the hat shop that I had hoped to skip breakfast altogether, but the garden looked inviting, and so I took my place at the wrought-iron table out on the grass and let Mrs. Hastings serve me, as it gave her great pleasure to do so.

It did not please me, however, that I was soon joined by Charles, who came around the side of the house and sat across from me. Nor did it escape me that for a man who was living elsewhere, he managed to show up regularly at mealtimes.

"Good morning," he said pleasantly, and then, waiting until Mrs. Hastings had served him his coffee and gone back inside, he said, "Tell me, Judith, what was the financial situation of your father at the time of his death? It seems inconceivable to me that he should die penniless as you would have us believe."

I could scarce believe his rudeness. "How can you doubt me?" I said. "What have I done to make you ask such a question?"

"I had not meant to be rude," he replied. "But as you are now considered family, you may be treated like family, and it's the type of question I would freely ask a sister."

Perhaps so, I thought. I could hardly expect to be embraced as family yet treated still as guest.

"Very well," I said. "My father did not have the business sense of Uncle Geoffrey, and some of his decisions were poor ones. While we did not live in poverty after his death, he owed so many people that Mother and I were forced to sell our most valuable possessions to pay off his debts."

"He left you nothing at all? Surely there was the family silver, your mother's jewelry, paintings, furnishings . . ."

"All that we had we sold, Cousin Charles. Mother and I moved into a set of rooms in a neighbor's house and lived very simply. And, simply put, I came to you penniless."

"Well, that is unfortunate, if true," said he. "Not, of course, that it makes any difference."

"Thank you," I said, wishing with all my heart that I could believe him.

I took another bite of biscuit, then a sip of tea, and when I looked up again I was disconcerted, for this time his frown had been replaced by a smile that was no more comforting, and his eyes were not on my face but on my figure.

I felt my cheeks burn and dropped my eyes once again. He laughed, and set down his cup. "Well, I see you are off to the gossip shop in your finery," he said. "Tell Violet Morrison that if she waggles her tongue any faster, the thing will fall off." And with that, he left the garden.

I will let no one ruin this day, I told myself

determinedly and, gathering up my plate and cup, took them into the house. Indeed, when I started out for the hat shop, the sun warm upon my face, the trees gloriously green—the green so new, the flowers so fresh, the breeze so light—I began to think that Whispers was the prettiest town on the east coast.

There were several customers inside the shop when I arrived, and before I knew it I was fetching the ribbon and thread for Helene, going in and out of the back room to get first one color of veiling, then another, and hoped most desperately to get through the day without a mistake.

Finally, at lunchtime, Violet and I went next door to the Bib and Bottle for a meat pie to eat on a bench outside. If only I could have taken off my slippers as well, I would have been content, for they were pointed at the ends and pinched my toes.

"Won't be too many days like this one," Violet said. "It'll be hotter than a stove lid come summer." She took a long drink of her ale, then asked me, "So what's it like living in the old Sparrow place?"

"I like it well enough," I told her. "I have a fine room overlooking the garden, and they ask very little of me. In short, I am treated as a daughter."

"But at night!" Violet went on, her eyes fastened on mine. "What do you do then?"

"What can you mean? I sleep, of course."

"Have you never seen or heard *her*?"

"Who?" I asked, but in my heart I knew the answer even before she spoke it, and gooseflesh arose on my arms.

"Jade Green," she answered. "She's there, they say. If you haven't seen her yet, you will."

Eight

I COULD HARDLY think, having heard from Violet's lips what I feared most.

Still, perhaps, this was the gossip Mrs. Hastings and Charles had both warned me about. Wasn't it human nature to suspect a ghost to reside in a house where a girl had died, especially one who had died by her own hand?

"Well," I said to Violet, "if Jade Green still haunts my uncle's house, I have yet to meet her."

And so we talked of other things, and it was a great relief to me when work was over for the day and I started the walk home, which would have been far more pleasant if I had worn more practical shoes.

I had not gone but half a block when the *clip clop* of horse's hooves slowed beside me, and I looked over to see Zeke Carey grinning at me from the wagon seat.

"Come on up," he said. "I'll drive you home."

"But it's a lovely day," I protested. "I can easily walk." In truth the wagon had never looked so good, and I longed to rest my feet.

"It's even lovelier up here," he said. "Besides, I have only one more delivery to make. Ride along with me and I'll show you the town."

That seemed a good enough reason to go, so I freely went over to the wagon and, with a hand from Zeke, hoisted myself onto the seat beside him. He gave the reins a shake, and off the horse started.

"You should get out in the air more," Zeke said to me, grinning still. "Your skin's as white as flour."

"It's always been so. I take after my mother," I told him.

"Work all day in a shop like that, your fingers will wither," he went on.

I only laughed. "The work suits me, and I like being out of my uncle's house during the day."

The horse trotted briskly along the winding road around the park, the tall trees, new with leaves, shading us as we rode.

"Down there is the pond," Zeke said, pointing. "We go ice-skating in the winter. And up ahead is the bandstand, and beyond that the town hall. I have a bag of cornmeal to deliver to the reverend, and then I'll show you the sea."

Well enough did I like sitting by the handsome boy who smelled vaguely of fresh perspiration, with apple on his breath. From the smile he gave me, I fancied he liked having me there. And so, perhaps because the cemetery we passed reminded me of Jade Green, I said to Zeke, "Have you heard of a girl named Jade Green?"

"Sure," he said. "Everyone knows about her. Why?"

"I wondered if you'd ever met her."

Zeke shook his head. "No. She was older than me, and sometimes I'd see her coming from the butcher shop, or going into the Bib and Bottle. She liked to stop there after work and have a pint, my brothers said. But I wasn't delivering for my father then—I was still in school."

"Violet Morrison tells me that my uncle's house is haunted," I said.

"I've heard that," Zeke replied. "But I don't believe in ghosts."

"Nor do I, but . . ." I stopped. "It's strange living in a house where there are things one cannot talk about, and where the color green is forbidden."

Zeke looked over at me, and this time he wasn't smiling. "If I were you, I would worry less about ghosts and more about your cousin Charles."

"But why?"

"No particular reason," he said. "Just keep it in mind."

We stopped at the reverend's house, and I held the reins while Zeke carried the large bag of cornmeal up the walk and around in back, balancing it on his broad shoulder, his blond hair bright in the afternoon sun. And then we were off again, the horse going at a steady clip, until we had crossed the main north–south road in Whispers and were traveling along the narrow lane that skirted the sea.

It was then I got my first glimpse of the ocean, and how I stared, for living as I had in Ohio, I was used to land about me in all directions and had never looked out across a body of water to see no trees or hills on the other side.

"It's beautiful, Zeke!" I gasped. "Look how the water rushes and swells! I did not know an ocean was so much a living thing!"

"You should see it in a storm," said Zeke. "There's a cove, though, where the water is calm, and I like to fish." He smiled. "You can come with me sometime and bait my hook."

"I'll do no such thing!" I told him, laughing, but to myself I said, Why not?

I had not thought anything of accepting the ride with Zeke Carey, but when the horse and wagon pulled up to the iron gate of my uncle's house, Uncle Geoffrey was waiting for me, Mrs. Hastings standing in the doorway behind him, looking anxious.

"What is it?" I asked, alighting from the wagon with the help of Zeke's strong arm as my uncle came forward to open the gate.

"You had us all worried about you!" said my uncle. "Mrs. Hastings thought you should have been home forty minutes ago, and when I went to inquire of Helene Harper, she told me you had left the shop at five."

"I'm truly sorry, Uncle!" I said. "I didn't think my lateness would cause you any alarm."

"I take full responsibility," Zeke apologized from the wagon seat. "It was I who persuaded her to come for a ride, and we should have stopped here first and told Mrs. Hastings we were going."

The cook waved her spoon in his direction. "That you ought, Zeke Carey! Don't you be going off with our Judith without telling us."

"Well, then, I may be driving her home again soon, so may I tell you now?" he said, bold as brass, and even my uncle had to smile.

I said a hasty good-bye to the mischievous fellow and went in the house, secretly glad that my uncle showed such concern for my welfare.

As I started up to my room, however, Mrs. Hastings stopped me on the landing. "Your uncle was in a terrible state, Judith. He feared something dreadful might have happened to you."

"Because of what happened to Jade Green?" I whispered back.

"I suppose so. Try not to make him worry."

"If I'm late again, it will be because I'm riding with Zeke," I said. And then, laughing, I added, "Truly, I am not about to take my own life. You need not worry one minute about that."

It did not seem to comfort her, though. "Other things could happen," she said darkly. "Just be watchful, child."

Again my body felt chilled as though a window had been left ajar, or a sudden draft had passed me on the stairs.

When Mrs. Hastings had gone back to the kitchen, I waited until I heard the clatter of her pots and pans, and then I went in the spare bedroom and sat down on the edge of Jade Green's bed, staring at the door to the attic.

Why did she do it? I wondered again. *How* did she

do it? I tried to imagine, were I so inclined, what I should use to do the deed. Finally, drawn to those bloodstained stairs, I reached for the door handle and once again turned the knob.

Instantly I jerked backward, my hands over my mouth, for there on the steps, the blood-soaked steps, lay a girl's white glove.

I could only sit and stare, my temples throbbing with fright. The glove was about the size of my own hand, certainly not large enough for Mrs. Hastings, and I knew positively it had not been there when I was in the attic last.

I steeled myself and, with trembling fingers, leaned forward and picked it up. And then I got my second shock, for beneath the glove was something else I had not noticed before—the deep cuts from a cleaver etched well into the wood of the step.

In terror, I tossed the glove back upon the attic stairs, closed the door, and fled to my room. Someone, I concluded, was playing tricks on me, and I vowed to put the death of Jade Green out of my mind. It had happened over three years ago, and it did no good to brood over what could not be undone. Let Uncle Geoffrey and Mrs. Hastings worry if they must, but it did not concern me.

When I had calmed myself at last, I set about

selecting my clothes for the following day. I'd noticed that both Helene and Violet dressed with care, their accessories perfectly chosen, and decided that I too would come to work each day dressed in my best.

I had just turned from my closet with a skirt upon my arm when, out of the corner of my eye, I saw something dart across the floor and under my dresser. I whirled around quickly, but too late to see what it was.

Immediately I took the mousetrap out of my closet and placed it under my dresser instead.

Dinner went as usual, with Charles having naught to say except that there were fine horses running at the racetrack, and Mrs. Hastings inquiring whether or not we were enjoying her pudding. I was afraid I would be lectured again about my ride with Zeke Carey, but it was not mentioned, and after dinner, when the dishes were washed and put away, I went into the parlor and played some songs for my uncle, being careful not to include "Springfield Mountain" among them.

As the doors were open and a breeze blew through the parlor, I felt in need of a wrap. I went upstairs and had just turned down the hall when I heard a soft oath from within my room, and a moment later a mousetrap came sliding out my door, across the floor, and into the wall opposite.

Imagine my surprise when Cousin Charles appeared next and, as startled to see me as I was to see him, made a quick apology and strode quickly down the hall to his own room.

I found my shawl and went out in the garden to consider the situation, trying to think what possible reason Charles could have had for putting his hand beneath my dresser. I remembered the question he had asked about my family's finances—his suspicion, perhaps, that I had come with a modest fortune I had hidden in my room—and began to suspect that my cousin was a thief, that he could only have been searching for the place I hid my wages.

I wondered if Mrs. Hastings suspected it too, for she later came out to walk with me and said, "About your wages, my girl. What will you do with the money you earn from the hat shop? It would be well, I think, for you to have a safe place to keep it."

"I haven't earned all that much yet, Mrs. Hastings, but when I do, I suppose I shall keep it in my desk," said I.

"You may do with it as you wish," she told me, "but I might suggest, for your own safety, that you give it to either your uncle or me to put away for you. Of course you may have it whenever you like."

"And so I shall," I promised, for she knew Charles better than I did.

Charles was aloof the rest of the evening. He said nothing at all to me by way of explanation, nor did he bid me good night when he left the house to go to his own lodgings.

I retired early, wanting to be at the shop on time the next morning, but awoke in the night not sure of the clock. I sensed that someone was in the room with me, however, and in my dreamlike state, thought perhaps it was already morning—that I had overslept, and Mrs. Hastings had come to fetch me.

I lay there waiting to hear her voice, when something touched my forehead.

"Yes?" I said sleepily. And then, turning slightly, I opened my eyes and found myself staring into darkness. "Yes?" I said again.

Suddenly I was very much awake. It was the middle of the night, and I could make out nothing but blackness.

"Who is it?" I whispered and, afraid it was Charles, I screamed.

For a moment nothing happened. Then I heard a thump across the hall, followed by another, doors opening, then footsteps. Finally, with her nightcap askew, Mrs. Hastings came into my room with a candle, followed soon after by Uncle Geoffrey.

I was breathing so rapidly, I could not talk. I lay curled against the headboard, blankets around me, cowering like a small animal about to be devoured.

"Gracious, child, what is it?" cried Mrs. Hastings, rushing over. "What is the matter?"

Looking about the room in all directions, I could see nothing. My first thought was to tell them I had suspected someone to be in my room, but if I did, Uncle Geoffrey would surely insist on checking it out—under my bed, in my closet . . . he might even look inside my trunk, lest someone be hiding there, and this I could not allow.

"It . . . it was only a dream," I said. "I'm sorry to have wakened you."

"Are you sure now?" asked my uncle.

"Yes. I've . . . I've had these dreams from time to time since my parents died. They come and go," I said.

"Oh, I know how it is," Mrs. Hastings told me. "After my Henry died, I had the same. You go back to sleep, dear, and I'll leave the candle burning on your dresser."

And so they left, but I dared not close my eyes. Fear gave way to anger. Someone *had* been in my room, I was sure, and I suspected it might have been Charles. It would be an easy thing for him to come in the night, unknown to us, and to slip out again as quickly as he had come. His lurking about, the glove upon the stairs, and now this—the touch of my forehead in the dead of night. Since he had not hurt me, he could only be trying to drive me mad, to insure that I would not receive any of the inheritance he felt to be his. I would rather believe he was trying to dislodge me of reason than to believe that my mind was, indeed, beginning to fail. If Charles was behind this, I told myself bravely, he would find me ready to fight.

I got up and, taking the candle, went downstairs to the kitchen. Opening first one drawer, then another, my fingers closed at last around a butcher knife. I took it upstairs and placed it in my bedside table.

Nine

S TRANGELY ENOUGH, I slept, convinced that either I had been dreaming or, were Charles still about, he would not chance awakening the household a second time with my screams. I vowed to keep the knife there in my room with me.

For the whole of that week, until the rain began on Friday, I took my breakfast outside in the garden, and managed to be reading a book whenever Charles arrived for his morning coffee, so that he was forced to converse with the cook, and I, when asked a question, answered him pleasantly enough and then went on with my reading.

I was most unsettled, then, the following week, at another vexing occurrence. I took a mild stomach flu, and so excused myself from the parlor after dinner and went to bed. While I was lying there in the gathering darkness, fully awake this time but with my eyes closed, I felt what seemed like fingers brush across my lips.

Gasping, I sat up, searching the room for the intruder, and reached for the knife in my bedside drawer. No one was there. My room was empty, and I was surprised to hear my cousin's voice downstairs, arguing again with his father. *Was* I going mad, then—hearing things, seeing things, and now feeling things that did not exist? Tears sprang to my eyes, for if I lost my reason, I should lose all.

I was sick the next day too, but the day after that, I was determined to go to the hat shop. Uncle Geoffrey called upon Zeke to come round and drive me, so that I would not tire myself unnecessarily.

"I hear you've been ill," said Zeke as we started off.

"I'm really quite fine now," I told him.

"I'm glad," said he, and I was surprised how much it cheered me to hear him say it.

He took the long way round just to show me the fishermen standing out in the surf, waiting for their morning catch. "Come to the cove with me sometime when the weather's hot," he said. "You'll like it."

"I might," I said, and wondered later, when he let me off at the shop, whether I only imagined it or if he had not held my hand longer than necessary to see me safely to the ground.

I wore a skirt of blue silk with a shirtwaist of the same color, and both Helene and Violet commented on my attire.

"Blue is definitely your color," Helene told me. "Either blue or green would go exceptionally well with your skin."

I thanked them for their remarks, glad that, if I did indeed look my best, I had appeared so in front of Zeke Carey.

"Is he your new beau?" asked Violet, as together we unpacked a shipment of tulle in the back room.

I blushed. "He's a friend who has been very kind to me," I told her politely. Violet, smiling, poked me in the ribs, and then we both broke into laughter.

"Truly, though," said Violet, "blue does become you, yet I never see you in green."

I lowered my voice and my eyes as well. "It is forbidden," I told her.

"What?"

"The color is not allowed in the Sparrow house. It was the condition given me for my coming."

Violet stopped her work and stared at me with her large dark eyes. "Then it must be because of *her!*" she insisted. "Jade Green! Green was *her* favorite color, and she wore it all the time."

"That's what I suspected," said I. "Perhaps it reminds my uncle too much of her."

But Violet shook her head. "I don't think that's it at all." She went to the doorway to check on the whereabouts of Helene and, seeing her with two customers over by the fitting table, she came back to me and whispered, "When one of our customers, Mrs. Tillis, died young—her dress caught fire—her husband married again within two months of her burial. He had given away all that belonged to her except for her favorite bonnet, which he had especially liked her to wear. And then the new bride took to wearing it, and before long, they say, the house was shaken with moans and sighs, until Mr. Tillis himself got rid of the hat."

"Oh, Violet, that surely must be gossip," I said quickly.

She shook her head and lowered her voice to a whisper. "They say that when someone dies a violent death, the ghost may appear at the place or dwelling, drawn by a favorite possession of the one who has died. A toy, for example, in the case of a child, or the familiar bed of an old man, or the bridal veil of a young woman. The favorite thing of Jade Green, we all knew, was a color."

My body grew chill at her words, remembering the hand that had twice brushed my face as I slept in my uncle's house. And yet, I reminded myself, that wasn't Jade Green's bed, for she had slept in the small spare room. No, my heart told me, if the ghost of Jade Green was about, it had been attracted to my room by the color green, the frame on my mother's picture. Perhaps my uncle too had heard the saying that Violet had related to me, and would take no chance of summoning the ghost.

"You're still looking a little ill," Violet said to me. "Are you sure you should have come back to work so soon?"

"I am quite well enough to work," I told her. "Suppose we finish unpacking this box, and then I'll practice my stitching."

My mind was in such turmoil, however, that I could scarce think of anything else that afternoon. Uncle did not seem a man given to superstition. Would he go to such lengths to ward off even the possibility of a ghost? All I could conclude was that the ghost of Jade Green was perhaps no stranger to the household, and it was for this reason that the house had been cleared of any reminder of her. Every reminder, perhaps, save the blood on the attic stairs, which even Mrs. Hastings had no great eagerness to ever look at again.

"No, no, Judith, I asked for the burgundy trim," I heard Helene saying, and I apologized profusely, determined to keep my mind upon my work, whatever should happen back in the Sparrow house.

When I got home that afternoon, Mrs. Hastings insisted I should rest, but I convinced her to let me walk in the garden. The sky was cloudy, the sun nowhere to be seen, but the air was warm, the vegetables and flowers were taking on new buds and blossoms, and the breeze had a feel of summer that assured me I was better off walking about here than lying abed in my room. The old gardener wordlessly pointed out a bush that was beginning to flower, and the scent was so sweet that I was soothed by its fragrance alone.

There were too many things troubling me, however, to forget my cares entirely. For one, I knew not how to respond to Charles anymore. When he arrived for dinner that evening, I studied him across the creamed chicken, and, noticing, he gave me a half smile that was more disquieting than comforting. I had been so convinced it was he who had been in my room, touching me in my bed, that I had screamed for Mrs. Hastings. And yet I was quite sure now I had been mistaken. One minute he seemed to tease me, like a fond brother, and then he would say something almost rude.

Perhaps this is the way with men and brothers, I thought. What would I know of their behavior, being an only child myself? Wasn't it right within a family that all should speak their minds freely, for if one cannot say what is in one's heart at the table, where then can he express himself? The way his eyes sought out my body, however—the way his fingers had once traced the buttons on my bodice—and Zeke's admonitions to be watchful of Charles . . . these all played upon my mind. I did not feel the trust one should feel toward a brother.

And yet I stayed quite jolly at mealtime, regaling my new family with stories of customers that came in the hat shop, the poodle that ate its mistress's bonnet, and so forth.

Mrs. Hastings laughed heartily, glad for some merriment, I fancied, over dinner, and I even saw a bemused smile on my uncle's face. Charles, for his part, told of going to the barber to have his hair trimmed, and there being a young boy having his curls removed for the very first time. He had pointed to his tresses there on the floor, said Charles, and wept, "Look at them! They're dead!"

We laughed again, and as I went upstairs later, I wondered if perhaps I had been wrong in all things about my family. But once in my room, an uneasiness overtook me, and I felt chilly despite the warmth of the evening. I tried sitting by the window to recapture the pleasure I had felt in the garden that afternoon, and yet I found myself turning repeatedly to look over my shoulder, sensing an unseen presence in the room. I do not know how I knew, for I heard nothing remarkable, felt no touch.

I shall bathe myself, I thought. *Perhaps that will calm me.* But this time, as I turned to get up, I gasped in horror, and my breath stopped. For there on my rug lay a hand, a human hand. A girl's right hand, detached from arm and body.

I slid back on the window seat until I was pressed against the glass, my hands covering my mouth. I tried to scream, but my breath was gone and no sound issued from my throat. I could only stare at the ghastly spectacle—the limp, white fingers, the delicate wrist, and then, the jagged stump on which dried blood was visible, the broken connection of bone and muscle and skin. . . .

More terrible still, the fingers suddenly began to

move, the palm to lift, until it was standing upright like some strange primordial creature.

Drawing my feet up beside me, I sat choking, shaking, as the fingers scrabbled swiftly along the floor, and the hand disappeared into the darkness beneath my bed.

Ten

I MADE NO move, uttered no sound, my body frozen to the chair.

Should I run for the door? I wondered. I imagined myself rushing downstairs to the parlor with an account of what I had just seen. Who would believe me? And what lay under the bed? The very body of the girl, perhaps? My teeth were chattering so violently that I had to hold my jaws to stop them.

As the minutes went by and nothing happened, I knew that I should—I *must*—gain courage enough to look under the bed itself before I summoned my uncle and Mrs. Hastings. If the corpse be there, I must warn them, for surely the shock, if it was close to claiming *my* sanity, might cost those two dear people their lives. I sat watching the floor, waiting, waiting for the hand to show itself again. But there was no noise, no movement.

Breathing rapidly, a trickle of perspiration running down the middle of my back, despite my chill, I slowly leaned down and picked up a corner of the bedspread, then bent over until I could see beneath the bed frame. It was dark under the bed, and I stared into the blackness, looking for any sign of white fingers, but saw nothing more.

What should I do? Whom should I tell? If it was indeed a ghostly hand belonging to Jade Green, my uncle would ask, *You didn't bring anything green into the house, did you?* I would have to admit my guilt, and would be turned out of his home, deservedly so. I was trapped.

Finally I got up enough nerve to light my candle and kneel beside my bed. The light flickered, casting a yellow glow on the floor. The space beneath my bed was empty. The hand had gone.

How was I to live here? How could I possibly sleep? To mention what I had seen to anyone at all, even Violet Morrison, might see me locked up as a madwoman, pitied and forgotten. And beneath this worry was the even greater one that perhaps there had been no hand at all, and my mind, like my mother's, betrayed me.

By morning, I had slept not more than a few minutes here, a few there, and I went down to breakfast groggy, my eyes puffy and red. Charles seemed amused at my discomfort.

"What's wrong, Orphan? You look a wreck!" he said. "Is something wrong with your bed, then?"

"No, I was just restless," I said. "I'm sure I shall sleep better tonight."

But Mrs. Hastings studied me over the porridge. "You shall, indeed, or I'll not have you working at the hat shop," she declared. "There's no need for it! If the work is too much for you, that will be that!"

This bothered me sorely, for I wanted to have a job, with spending money of my own. I wanted to be friends with Violet, and do other things besides sit at home, no matter how fond I was of the cook. My worry and lack of sleep upset me even more, for if I did not do a good job for Helene, she would let me go.

I struggled through the morning as best I could, and was disappointed at lunchtime when it rained and Violet and I could not sit on the bench outdoors in the sun.

"Tell you what," said Violet. "I'll go next door and

get our meat pies, and we'll eat them back here. Helene goes to the bank on Fridays, so we shall have the place to ourselves. We can be grand ladies come to purchase bonnets, and try on every hat in the shop if we like."

I smiled at her plan in spite of myself, and was quite ready to sit down when she returned. We spread a cloth on a table in the back room, turned the sign at the window so customers should not interrupt our lunch, then settled down to eat and talk while rain streamed down the windows and beat on the roof.

"Lordy, it's a right good blow!" Violet declared, looking out the window as she ate. "Almost like a hurricane. We see plenty of those here in Whispers. Wouldn't mind a bit if I never saw one again."

We finished the pies and debated whether to go back to the Bib and Bottle for biscuits and ale, when we decided it was not fit weather to go out again.

"Helene is probably stranded at the bank. If she goes out in this, she'll ruin her silk," said Violet. "So what shall we do till she gets back?" And then, mischievously, she added, "We could always tell ghost stories."

"I think not," I told her. "I've trouble enough sleeping in my uncle's house."

"Why?" asked Violet with a grin. "Do you hear moans and rattling chains?"

"No, I hear nothing like that."

"Cries and whispers?"

"No, nor that." And suddenly I asked, "Violet, do you know why Jade Green killed herself? Did anyone ever find that out?"

Violet shook her head and brushed the crumbs from her dress. "She left no note, nor did she tell any secrets. It was the greatest shock, they say, to Mrs. Hastings, as she expected nothing of the sort from her."

"Did . . . did anyone ever tell you how she took her life? Was it poison?" I was thinking of the words to "Springfield Mountain," her favorite song.

Here Violet lowered her voice though we were the only two in the shop. "That is strangest of all, Judith, and the last way in this world I should ever want to kill myself."

"How?"

"She bled to death. Cut off her own hand."

I clutched my stomach.

"Horrible, isn't it? They say she bled all over the floor." And then, looking at me, she cried, "Judith, you are as pale as cream! I shouldn't have told you! You have to live there, after all."

"It's all right," I assured her. "It's something I would have found out anyway."

But all the while my fingers and toes had gone cold as ice.

I wanted to busy myself as soon as possible, so I began my afternoon's work. Helene came in at last and said she had met Zeke at the livery stable and that he would come by for me at five o'clock, with an umbrella to shield me, and I was very glad to hear it.

When the day was over, however, and I climbed in the wagon, the rain had stopped and there was no need of umbrella, though gray clouds swirled overhead. I was so nervous, though, that everything seemed to me a bad omen.

"Zeke," I said, feeling distraught. "I would ask a favor of you."

"Of course," said he.

"Meet me at the back of the garden by the alley in a half hour's time; there is something I want to give you," I told him.

He glanced at me with a surprised smile. "How can I refuse a gift?" he asked.

"Promise you'll come!" I pleaded.

He looked at me more strangely still. "Of course. What's the matter, Judith?"

I tried to be gay. "Nothing!" I said, with a small

86

laugh. "I just want to give you a gift for driving me home."

He let me out at my uncle's gate, and I hurried up the walk and steps to the door. Once inside, I called to Mrs. Hastings that I would have my tea with her shortly, then ran immediately upstairs.

Every time I opened my closet, I did so now with great trepidation, and as I put my hand upon the doorknob, I braced myself for what I might see. My room was no longer a safe retreat, a refuge from the cares of the day, and if I was to stay in Whispers, this could not continue. I knew I must rid myself of the picture frame my mother had given me, dear as it was, so that once again there would be peace in my uncle's house.

I took a deep breath and turned the knob, my eyes on the floor of the closet, searching for the severed hand. But nothing seemed amiss, and—my courage bolstered—I crawled to the back of the closet beneath the eaves and opened the lid of the trunk.

All appeared as it should be, and I decided it was time to remove my summer frocks anyway. So I set to work, lifting them out one by one and placing them on the floor beside me. The framed photo was just as I had left it, lying facedown on the bottom of the trunk.

Picking it up in one hand, my dresses in the other, I backed out of the closet and laid my clothes over a chair. Then I wiped the frame on my skirt and, turning the photo over, choked back a scream. For I saw not the gentle face of my mother but the face of a stranger, a girl my own age in a cotton dress, her eyes set in a saucy stare.

I threw the picture onto the bed in fright, one hand on my chest. Jade Green! It had to be. She had taken over my frame, my trunk, my room, and, for all I knew, my mind. I knew not where it would end.

Wrapping my arms about my body, I leaned trembling against the wall. Finally, however, mindful that Zeke was waiting for me at the back of the garden, I once more gathered my wits about me. A picture is only a picture, I told myself, and went over to retrieve the frame and remove the photograph within. When next I looked, however, it was a photograph of my mother once again.

My breath came short in faint little gasps. I slipped the picture of my mother out of its frame and put it back in the trunk. Then I searched through my box of photographs until I found one of myself of the proper size, taken when I was ten. It was not at all a good likeness, but it was all that would fit. I put it in the frame.

Running one finger lovingly over the green silk, I wrapped the framed picture in tissue and went downstairs, hiding my parcel in the folds of my skirt.

"The water's boiling, Judith. Have some tea," called Mrs. Hastings.

"In a while," I called back. "Zeke gave me a ride home this afternoon, when my legs needed a walk instead. I'd like to stroll the garden first, and then we can have our tea."

She came out into the sunroom where I was preparing to open the door. "It's muddy out there, my girl. You'd best watch where you step."

"I will," I told her. And then I went outside and walked through the hedgerows until I was out of sight of the house.

The garden stretched a long way back, ending at the alley, and I began to hurry, anxious to get rid of the frame that had caused so much distress to me. Never did I think I would part with the gift my mother had given me, but I knew I could not live with the ghostly hand in the house. The longer I clutched the frame, the more desperately I longed to be rid of it, and soon I began to run, unmindful of puddles, slipping and sliding along the muddy path in the maze of hedgerows, until I came to a corner and, turning swiftly, ran right into my cousin Charles.

Eleven

H<small>E CAUGHT</small> my wrist and held me there while I strove desperately with my other hand to keep my small parcel hidden behind me.

"Aha!" cried he, his eyes laughing. "And where would our orphan be off to?" He swung me about so I was facing him. "See? Your cheeks are so pink, you must be going to meet a lover."

"I have no lover," I told him. "I was just going for a walk in the garden."

Charles pulled me closer, though I bid my feet remain where they were.

"That was no walk, Orphan, that was a run!"

he said. "How eager you are! And if you've no lover, how about a kiss for your cousin?"

"No, Charles!" I said, trying to pull away from him. "Please . . ."

His grip tightened even more on my hand, however, as though to pull me down, yet I gave a little cry, "No! Stop!" and swung at him lightly with the picture frame.

There were footsteps coming up the path from the alley, then Zeke's voice: "Judith? Where are you? What's wrong?"

Instantly Charles released my hand.

"Aha!" said he again. "You *were* going to meet a lover. And what do you have there? My family's silver? Robbing my father behind his back?"

"No!" I cried, just as Zeke came around the hedgerows.

Charles gave us both a scornful look and straightened up. "Good day," he said stiffly to Zeke, and went quickly up the path to the house. I knew not what he would tell my uncle.

I grabbed Zeke's hand and hurried on down to the alley so as not to be overheard.

"What was happening?" he asked me. "What's wrong?"

I tried to dismiss it. "It was only Charles being

Charles," I told him. And then, trying to put a natural face on a day that was unnatural in the extreme, I presented him the parcel in tissue paper. "Please keep this for me, Zeke," I said. "And thank you for being so kind."

Puzzled, he stared down at the package, then took it in his hands and slowly unwrapped the tissue. After what had taken place in my bedroom, I didn't know what he would see when he examined the frame. But there was my photograph at ten years of age, just as I'd wrapped it.

He stared at it hard as the color rose in my cheeks. Finally he asked, "Judith, is this you?"

"Yes," I said, feeling most awkward. "It . . . it's all I have just now. All that would fit the frame. It was taken when I was ten."

The more words tumbled from my lips, the more ridiculous they sounded, but parting with the frame itself gave me the greatest distress. I could scarcely let go of it.

"I hope you didn't feel you had to give me something merely because I wanted to drive you home," he said. "But I'll keep it always, of course."

And as though I had not been awkward enough already, I said, "Oh, you don't have to keep it forever; you can always give it back after . . . after . . ."

92

Too confused and embarrassed to describe, I turned and fled back up the path like a silly child of six and burst into Mrs. Hastings' kitchen, my cheeks aflame.

"Well, goodness, what is this?" she said. "Have you taken a fever, my girl?"

To add to my embarrassment, she was pouring tea for Charles, who sat solemnly at the table, watching me as I took my seat.

"She's a gadabout, Mrs. Hastings," he said. "Here, there . . . meeting young men at the back of the garden."

"What?" Mrs. Hastings put down the sugar and looked at me.

"It was only Zeke," I said.

"I've nothing against Zeke Carey," said Mrs. Hastings. "But why couldn't he come to the door, Judith?"

"Why not, indeed?" exclaimed Charles. Oh, how I disliked him then, to imply such things of me, and in front of Mrs. Hastings too.

"Well," said she, "let's have no more meetings at the back of the garden, my girl. Let him sit in the parlor the way young men are taught to do when they come courting. To meet him in the alley will only cause people to talk, and"—Here she paused, hand on the creamer—"we *all* know how reputations can be ruined by talk," she said, looking right at Charles.

He held his tongue, but I was too miserable to take tea any longer and, claiming a headache, went upstairs.

As I passed the doorway to Jade Green's old bedroom, I paused, staring hard at the attic door until I could gather up my courage. Then I swiftly walked into the room, around the bed, and jerked open the narrow door. The glove was gone. The stairs were empty, except for the bloodstain.

Back in my own room, I lay down on the bed and mulled over all that had happened. With Charles about, he could well have put the glove on the attic stairs for me to find, and could easily have taken it away. That did not explain the hand, of course—the ghastly, ghostly hand. But at last I had rid the house of the picture frame, and were I to be asked now, I could truly say that there was nothing green in my room or on my person or on any of my possessions whatsoever.

As my body relaxed, I listened to the sounds around me—Mrs. Hastings' voice far off in the kitchen, the sound of a carriage out on the street, the twitterings of birds. There was no noise at all from my closet.

At dinner I felt better, and looked forward to the

roast lamb that Mrs. Hastings had set before us. I was telling Uncle Geoffrey about how dreadfully hard it had rained at lunchtime, and how I should not go off again without an umbrella.

I was shocked to hear Cousin Charles interrupt me then to say, "Better watch her, Father. She'll go out of this house with more than an umbrella. It wouldn't surprise me a bit if she were taking away the family silver."

"Charles!" cried Mrs. Hastings.

I was too stunned to reply.

Uncle Geoffrey put down his wineglass. "And on what do you base that accusation, Charles?" he asked.

"I caught her running through the garden toward the alley this afternoon, Father. She was looking very guilty, very flushed, and had a parcel hidden in her skirt. I tried to question her, but she broke away and ran to meet Zeke Carey. When she returned, she came empty-handed."

I was close to tears, but so angry, it was all I could do to speak: "Are you accusing me of stealing, sir?" I asked, looking directly at Charles, my voice shaking.

"I didn't say you were, Cousin. I said you bear watching, that's all," he replied.

Mrs. Hastings looked at me questioningly. "What you give to Zeke is your business, my girl, but—"

"It was a picture," I blurted out quickly, my face aflame. "A picture of me. Nothing more."

"You gave him your picture, Judith?" inquired Mrs. Hastings, more surprised than angry. "Well, now!" She smiled just a little. "I say!"

Uncle Geoffrey's voice took over the table then. "You spoke quite correctly, Emma. It is Judith's business, not ours, and I do not wish to hear any more about it. And Charles, since you yourself profess to abhor gossip, I trust you will not supply us with any more at the table in the future."

Charles's face expressed no emotion, but I was most surprised and grateful to hear Uncle Geoffrey take my part. Indeed, I had been noticing lately a small change in my uncle—a smile that brightened his face whenever I entered the room. Little inquiries now and then about my health, my comfort, my likes and dislikes. I could tell that he looked forward immensely to the parlor after dinner when I played for him some of his favorite songs, the setting sun coming through the stained-glass panel above the side window, making a rainbow of color on the wall.

Mrs. Hastings too had her favorites and, when the dishes were done and the floor swept, she would often join us with her embroidery, slip off her shoes, and request a song, which I would attempt to play for her on the piano. Sometimes she would even hum along.

It was nighttime I dreaded, though. I knew that I would soon be able to tell whether I had driven the hand—that macabre horror of a hand—from the house by ridding my room of the green picture frame, or whether Jade Green was still with us.

And so, after Charles had left that evening and Uncle Geoffrey began closing the windows downstairs, I bid him and Mrs. Hastings good night and went up to my room.

The air was warm—too warm, almost, for a sheet—and I lay in my gown with only my feet lightly covered. Just as I had that afternoon, I listened for any sound at all in my room—any scratching, scurrying, rustles, or creaks.

There was nothing at all, and I thought what a mercy it would be if, in ridding the Sparrow house of green, I were ridding it of Jade as well.

I tried not to think of Charles and how I had angered him that afternoon by refusing his kiss. How he, in turn, had made such terrible accusations in front of his father and Mrs. Hastings. It seemed we should always be enemies.

I soon found myself drifting off in the most delicious sleep, however, and when I half wakened once or twice, the sleep, the bed, my pillow all felt so comfortable that I gave myself over to them again and again.

But sometime in the night, perhaps two or three, I was drawn slowly back to consciousness by the sound of music.

Could I be dreaming still? I wondered. Were there revelers outside my window, coming home from a party? Or was it morning already, with Mrs. Hastings singing as she made the biscuits?

As I came further awake, I realized it was not a voice at all but rather a simple melody, and the words to the tune ran through my head:

Too roo de nay, too roo de noo.
Too roo de nay, too roo de noo.

Twelve

M Y BODY turned so cold upon hearing that song that I began to shake most violently. It was not coming from within my closet, or my room, but from somewhere far distant in the house. Frightened as I was, I had to know.

I got out of bed and, lighting my candle, carried it to the door.

"Too roo de nay, too roo de noo . . ." came the melody from the floor below. I went out into the hall. Was I the only one who could hear it?

Slowly I descended the long staircase, holding the candle far out in front of me to light my path, not my face. More slowly still, I crossed the hall when I reached the bottom and entered the parlor.

The moonlight through the window illuminated the rose-colored chair by the writing table, the brandy cupboard, the cushions, the clock. It shone as well on the grand piano, and, taking another step so as to get a closer look, I saw the hand, the severed hand, fingering the keys.

The music stopped and the hand turned, as though looking at me. With a small cry I fled the room. Still holding the candle, I stumbled up the stairs, tripping over my gown.

"Too roo de nay, too roo de noo," came the last strains of the song. And then all was still.

In bed at last, my head beneath the covers, I hugged myself to keep from shaking. I heard other footsteps in the hall, the low voice of Uncle Geoffrey, a door opening, then murmurs from Mrs. Hastings. The footsteps came toward my room and stopped outside my door. But finally, they returned from whence they'd come, and the house fell quiet again.

For me, however, it did not seem there would ever be peace again. I had wakened the ghost of Jade Green by bringing her color in along with my trunk, and now, it seemed, I had loosed her upon the house. Whatever would become of us, only the Lord knew.

The following day being Sunday, I stayed in bed late, having slept so poorly toward the end of the night, and came down to find Mrs. Hastings and my uncle having their breakfast out in the garden. Charles rarely came in time for breakfast on Sundays, and I looked forward to this one morning of the week I was free of my cousin's looks and comments. This time, however, still shaky from the events of the previous night, I would have preferred eating alone. But Mrs. Hastings saw me in the kitchen and motioned me to join them.

I took my muffin out to the table and sat down beside my uncle.

"Good morning, Uncle Geoffrey," said I. "And you also, Mrs. Hastings."

"A pleasant good morning to you, my girl," she replied, studying my face. "And how did you sleep?"

"It was a fitful night, but I managed," I replied.

Uncle Geoffrey was watching me also. "Has it ever been said, Judith, that you've been given to sleep-walking? That you, perhaps, walk about in your sleep and do things you might not remember doing in the morning?"

I tried to make light of it. "If I did, Uncle, I'm sure I should be the last to know."

"You do not remember going downstairs last night and playing a song on the piano?"

"How should I remember if I had?" I asked. "But why do you ask?"

"Only that we both seemed to have heard the piano playing last night, and also the floor creaking down at your end of the hall. When we came out to see, however, your door was closed and you were abed," said Mrs. Hastings. And then, turning to my uncle, she added, "Well, Mr. Sparrow, perhaps old age is catching up with us, eh, and we're imagining things?"

How I wanted to tell the dear woman that she was not mistaken at all, that it had not been I at the piano, but the ghostly hand of Jade Green. Yet I could not bring myself to do it, for I would have had to confess the green picture frame I'd brought into the house. Coward that I was, I feared I should then be turned out of the only home I knew.

In the days that followed, I heard no more music at night, nor did I see the hand. Indeed, summer had burst upon Whispers in such a profusion of flowers, a burst of heat, a blanket of humidity that I felt myself to be in a jungle. At the hat shop, Violet and I worked with front and back doors open so as to provide a breeze. Violet was teaching me to sew on a hatband without the stitches showing, and I took pride in needlework almost as fine as hers.

One Sunday Zeke stopped by and invited me to accompany him to the cove to do some fishing. I wondered he should ever want to see me again, so silly had I been in the garden the day I gave him my picture. But he insisted I come, and Mrs. Hastings said it would do me good. She advised me to wear my oldest frock, and gave me her rubber bathing sandals, that I might protect my feet upon the rocks.

"And take a parasol, my dear, to shade your skin from the sun," she said.

We intended to walk to the ocean this time, and appeared to be going on expedition, with fishing gear, picnic hamper, parasol, blanket, and sandals.

"You seem in a good mood!" Zeke said to me as we sauntered along the shady street.

"I am. I think I am in a better mood today than I have been since I came to Whispers," said I.

That pleased him, I could tell.

"Then I must be the one who has caused it," he said, smiling.

"You?" I cried, laughing. "And what has it to do with you?"

"Why, think how disappointed you are when I'm not there to drive you home in the wagon! How your face lights up when you see me coming!"

"It doesn't!" I said, swinging the parasol at him.

But then, as we turned the corner off onto a narrow dirt lane, our shoulders brushed together as we walked, and Zeke made no effort to pull away, nor did I. I thought how very true he spoke, and we grew quiet, not with awkwardness but with the pleasure of being together. Away from the Sparrow house, I strove to forget the hand, and there were even times I almost convinced myself that I had imagined it. Almost, but not quite.

The cove was back from the ocean, so that the rocks near the water's edge took the brunt of the pounding waves. But once they broke, the water rolled more languidly into the cove, and there it shimmered peacefully in the afternoon sun as gulls soared overhead and the ocean breeze fanned my face. Was there ever a place more lovely than this? I wondered.

For a time Zeke fished, and I made a willing audience as he showed me his lures. In the first hour he caught two fish—one for each of us, he said—but then I wandered off, climbing barefoot over the moss-covered rocks, lying facedown on their cool surface to explore the dark crevasses between them with my hand. Mrs. Hastings' rubber slippers proved too large for me, and one came off and was washed out into the surf.

I could not help laughing as Zeke propped his

fishing pole in the sand and went galloping out in the water to retrieve it, his trousers soaked. When he returned it to me, his clothes dripping, I was bent double with laughter, and the next I knew I was in his arms and he took me out in the water, despite my laughing screams, and dunked me in the surf.

Breaking free of him, my clothes clinging to my body, I splashed back to shore, Zeke behind me, where we collapsed on the blanket.

I was wringing out the hem of my dress, wiping my bare legs with my hand, when I happened to glance up at the rocks above and was startled to see Cousin Charles looking grimly down at us.

I was too surprised to say anything. He said nothing, either. With narrowed eyes, he simply observed me there on the blanket with Zeke, and then he walked away.

Thirteen

Z EKE," I said, turning. "He frightens me! Did you see the way Charles was looking at us up there?"

"At you more than me," Zeke said.

"I don't like the way he studies me sometimes. It's not right for a cousin."

"Then you should tell him straight out," said Zeke. "Don't be shy about it." He opened the picnic hamper. "Here. Let's see what Mrs. Hastings has packed for our lunch." He handed me a boiled egg and some dark bread, and soon we were settled against a rock, our bare feet thrust out in front of us, enjoying our lunch and the breeze that blew in off the water.

At that moment I wished I could stay there the rest of my life, so comfortable was I with Zeke, with the sand and the sun and the ocean. I could feel my skirt flopping about my legs in the breeze, drying against my thighs, and cared not at all that Zeke could see my ankles. I delighted, in fact, in the arch of my foot, the length of my toes, and thought how Mrs. Hastings would cluck her tongue if she saw me now.

"How long have you known my cousin Charles?" I asked suddenly.

"I've known the Sparrow family ever since I can remember," Zeke answered. "I knew who Charles was if I saw him on the street, but I never had much to say to him, or he to me. He's more than twice my age."

"Then, if you never really knew him, why did you dislike him and warn me, even before I told you how he affected me?" I inquired.

"His reputation, mostly," said Zeke.

"What sort of reputation is that?" asked I.

"Not the sort his father has, that's certain," Zeke said. And then he suggested we share the raspberry tea cake that was in the basket, and so the afternoon was blissfully whiled away. I lay on the blanket allowing my dress to dry, and Zeke continued fishing, though he caught nothing more.

About three o'clock, dark clouds appeared far

out over the ocean and came rolling in, as though riding the waves. We packed up for the journey home. For a moment, as we picked up the blanket, our hands touched. When Zeke brought his ends of the cloth toward mine, they touched again, and next, our lips.

That kiss, my very first from a man not my father, was as delicious as any tea cake I had ever tasted, which only made me hunger for more.

But Zeke drew away then, and, touching my hair, said, "Why did you give me a picture of yourself at ten? Why not a likeness of you as you are now?"

"It . . . it was all I had that would fit the frame," I said, blushing. "Someday I'll give you a better one."

"I'd rather the picture than the frame," said he.

Oh, how I wanted at that moment to tell him everything—to bare my soul of all I had seen and heard in the Sparrow house! And yet, something stopped me. Only I knew the enormity of what I had done by bringing back the color green against my uncle's wishes.

And so we walked home, Zeke giving my hand a squeeze before he sent me inside. And though the clouds brought rain, a drenching summer storm, my heart was filled with the delight of the afternoon, and I dared anyone to destroy it.

Either it was the happiness upon my face or a change in my uncle, I knew not, but after dinner that evening, he said, "Judith, how about a game of checkers in the parlor?"

"But I don't believe I have ever played," I told him.

"Then I'll teach you," said he, with pleasure. And then, more teasing, "I submit that there was a time you knew no songs, but someone taught you those as well."

And so, with Mrs. Hastings fanning herself by the window, I sat with my uncle learning the game of checkers, and it was not long before one of my men was crowned, then another, so that I had two kings upon the board.

"Aha!" cried Uncle. "For a girl who has never played, Judith, you are giving me a regular fight."

Charles, over on the sofa, watched for a time, then asked, "Have we given up the art of conversation for checkers, then?"

"I'll talk with you," said Mrs. Hastings genially. "Tell me, Charles, how would you cure a sleepwalker?"

I was not at all pleased with this turn in the conversation, but I frowned at the board before me and moved one of my men to the left.

"A sleepwalker, eh?" said Charles. "And what does this sleepwalker do?"

"That we will know eventually, I'll wager, but as

yet, she has come down the stairs and played a tune on the piano," said Mrs. Hastings.

I knew by the tone of her voice that it was only fond teasing on her part, yet I could not help but wonder why she brought this up with Charles, and could only guess that it still weighed some upon her mind—that she hoped each time the subject was aired she might convince herself that I had been the piano player. Had she herself suspicions that the ghost of Jade Green might be lurking about, or was it mere superstition that made her avoid the subject?

Charles, however, glancing only once in my direction, said, "Well, Mrs. Hastings, perhaps the solution is to lock the offender up. After all, she may fall down the stairs and break her neck. She might go to the stove and set the house afire. Put her in her room at nine o'clock each evening, lock the door, and keep the key in your nightdress until seven the next day."

The malice in his words did not escape Mrs. Hastings, for she said quickly, "Oh, that is too drastic a solution, Charles." And she laughed as though it were all a joke.

Uncle Geoffrey said, "Now Judith, you're not paying attention." And I saw I had moved a man in such a way that my uncle jumped three, capturing them all.

. . .

At work the next day, I said to Violet, "What do you know of my cousin Charles? You have lived here in Whispers all your life. What do they say about him around town?"

Violet rolled her eyes in the direction of Helene, and I knew that this too was not a topic of conversation to be discussed in the shop. So at noon, once again, when we ate our lunches out on the bench, sharing between us a small box of berries, she said, "If you want the truth about your cousin Charles, ask the ladies."

"What ladies?" said I, looking about.

Violet gave a laugh. "You won't see them now, Love, for they don't get up till six in the evening. The ladies of the night, I'm talking of."

I gasped. "You mean . . .?"

She smiled and nodded her head. "*Those* are the sort of ladies your cousin is out with. Why do you think he keeps rooms in town? Why, his father would throw him out he ever brought *that* sort home with him."

"And everyone knows this?"

"Almost everyone. But there's nothing to be done about it, is there? I mean, he's a man of forty—he can do what he likes."

I almost wished I had not heard what Violet told me, but I had asked for gossip, and gossip was what I

111

got. It did not make me feel any more kindly toward my cousin, though. In fact, at the dinner table that evening, I felt a great revulsion toward him, which I was sure he could sense from his chair at the end of the table.

"And what has our orphan been up to, that she's so quiet this evening?" he asked, feigning friendliness. "Was she climbing about on the rocks with her panting beau in pursuit? Was she slithering her naked foot up and down the length of his leg? Was she lying in the waves so that her clothes—"

"Charles, that's enough!" boomed his father suddenly. "Stop this! I will not stand for this sort of comment at my table."

All three of us stopped eating, for we had never seen Uncle Geoffrey look quite so angry, his face a deep purple. "If you have accusations to make, make them boldly, but by god, they had better be of such nature as to warrant our attention. Judith is not a prisoner here. She is allowed both her friends and her freedom, and if I may say, sir, you should be the last to impugn a person's character."

I truly expected a loud and lengthy argument to follow. Mrs. Hastings, in fact, got up quickly and made some excuse to attend to the kitchen, but Charles, surprisingly, apologized.

"What was mere joking was taken far too seriously, and I withdraw all my remarks thus far," he said, then lifted his wineglass and took a drink.

I looked quickly at my cousin's face but could not tell from his eyes whether he spoke with sincerity or sarcasm. His apology mollified my uncle, however, so that the rest of the meal passed pleasantly enough. When the apple tart was brought to the table later, we each ate a piece with many a compliment to the cook.

Charles left soon after dinner.

"Mrs. Hastings," I said. "It's a warm evening, and you are still flushed from cooking dinner. Why don't you and Uncle Geoffrey go out in the garden and let me set the kitchen to rights? I insist upon it."

She was still fanning herself, and I could see that my offer appealed to her.

"Go!" I said again. "The yellow rosebush far back by the gate is in bloom, and you should not miss it."

"Then I shall go!" Mrs. Hastings replied, getting out of her chair.

"The yellow rose?" inquired my uncle. "Of all the flowers, that is my favorite."

And so they went. I rolled up my sleeves and set about washing the pots and pans, rinsing the silver, and taking the unused potatoes and onions down to the root cellar.

I was just coming back up when I heard a noise in the kitchen. It was a familiar sound, as though Mrs. Hastings had returned and was starting to make dinner all over again.

Charles? I thought. Had he come back, and was rummaging about?

I got to the top step and stopped, listening.

Chop, chop, chop, the noise went.

"Mrs. Hastings?" I called.

The sound ceased for a moment.

I stepped up into the kitchen and looked about. Out the window I could see Mrs. Hastings and Uncle Geoffrey enjoying the garden. I glanced to my right, waiting for the sound to begin again, then to my left. *Chop, chop, chop.* I whirled about as the noise seemed to be coming from a back corner.

There on the chopping block was a cleaver, methodically hitting the board, rhythmically chopping. And grasping the cleaver was the ghostly hand.

Fourteen

I EDGED OUT of the kitchen and into the sunroom, stepping, it seemed, in time to the *chop, chop, chop* of the cleaver. I knew not whether to call for my uncle or run from the house, and surprised even myself that I did not scream. I stood, instead, waiting for the chopping to stop.

It did at last, just as the piano playing had commenced, then ended, and when at last I peeked into the kitchen, the hand was gone and the cleaver lay where Mrs. Hastings had left it. There were, however, new cuts on the chopping block, freshly made, and the depth of the cuts spoke even more of the strength that lay in that hand.

What did it mean? Was I to go on living like this the rest of my life, never knowing where the severed hand would next show itself, or what it might do? If it could hold a cleaver and bring it down with such force, were any of us safe?

Strangely, as frightened as I was of the apparition, I could feel an anger growing inside me, and a determination to catch this wayward hand and return it to its grave. If it was I who had awakened the ghost by bringing my mother's picture frame into the house, then it was I who should get rid of it, and that I made up my mind to do.

My uncle and Mrs. Hastings had evidently found the evening air much to their liking, and stayed out in the garden for some time, looking at first this flower, then another, while I cleaned the kitchen. I worked furiously, scouring, sweeping, soaping, rinsing, for my thoughts were all a tumble, and I did not know if my fervent activity was due more to anger or terror. Nonetheless, when I went out at last to join my uncle, I said, "Uncle Geoffrey, I'm afraid we might have rats, and I would like some traps to set about."

"Rats?" cried Mrs. Hastings. "Surely not!"

"I have seen some signs," said I. "Droppings, and

holes in the root cellar the size of tennis balls. If you'll get traps for me, I know right where to put them, for if there are rats in the cellar, they must be elsewhere in the house too."

"If we have rats, we will make short work of them," said my uncle. "I'll ask Zeke Carey to bring us traps tomorrow."

I wonder that I slept at all that evening. If Jade Green had cut off her own hand with a meat cleaver, what might she do to me? Was I in her favor or disfavor for letting her back into this house? At times my answer was that if she had meant to harm me, well might she have done so already. But the argument ran that perhaps she liked to toy with me first, even to drive me mad. Yet why? Why had she left in so terrible a manner, and for what reason had she returned?

The following day the rattraps were delivered, and the day after that, when Zeke was waiting for me with his horse and wagon outside Helene's Hat Shoppe, I climbed up beside him and said, "I would like to go to the cemetery, Zeke. I'd like to see the grave of Jade Green."

"Now that's a morbid thought for so beautiful a day," he said.

"I just want to see where she's buried," I told him.

It was as good an excuse as any to take me riding, Zeke probably thought, for he turned the horse in that direction and off we went. As we entered the gates of the graveyard, though, Zeke said, "You know, Judith, there are times I worry about you."

"Why?"

"The way you brood about Jade Green, for one."

His words disturbed me, that he should think me odd. Had he seen some trace of my mother's madness in me, something of which I myself was unaware? How glad I was I had not told him what I had seen so far in the house.

"Is that all that troubles you about me?" I asked.

"That . . . and other things," he said.

"*What* other things?" I questioned.

"Well, the picture you gave me—of you at ten."

"If you don't want it, Zeke, then give it back."

"You don't understand what I'm saying!" he insisted. "You were upset that night—like a desperate girl wanting to rid herself of the pox. What is it you're not telling me, Judith? There's more to the story, of that I'm sure."

His words were all true, yet I wanted Zeke to think only the best of me. So I told him that it was a strain living in a house where a girl had once taken her life, and that perhaps when I saw where she was buried, I could put the matter to rest and forget about Jade Green. Zeke seemed to accept this as reasonable. What would he think of me, I wondered, if he knew that I was planning to capture a severed hand and bury it here on top of the grave where it belonged?

The sky had been gray that morning, and continued gray even now, clouds billowing overhead like froth in a soup kettle. For some time we rode in silence, and then Zeke said, "My father saw your cousin in the Bib and Bottle last night. The way Charles was talking, it seemed he would have people believe that your uncle is becoming senile."

"Why on earth would he talk so?" I exclaimed. "Indeed, Uncle has all his faculties about him, and I have never noticed him to forget the slightest detail. He keeps every appointment, arriving on time, and attends to his obligations better than most of us."

"That was how my father answered him, that if Geoffrey Sparrow were becoming senile, then there was no hope for the rest of us, for he is as punctual as a clock, as sharp as a pin."

I was puzzled, though, that Charles would tell such a lie. "For what purpose would a man tell a falsehood about his own father?" I asked.

"That's what I asked *my* father," said Zeke. "He tells me that if your uncle were to be declared incompetent by the court at some time in the future, Charles would inherit his estate, being his only living heir. With the exception of you, of course."

"Me? I am only his niece," I replied.

"But an heir, nonetheless. It all depends on what your uncle has written in his will. Regardless of what the will says, though, my father tells me, if your cousin can convince the court that it should be declared invalid because your uncle was not himself when he wrote it, then Charles stands to gain a great deal."

I did not like to hear this talk, for it saddened me to think of Uncle passing away. Should that happen, I'm convinced, my cousin would have me barred from his house without a penny to my name.

I sat thinking how I should save every cent I earned toward the day when this might happen. I had been doing as Mrs. Hastings advised, turning over the greater part of my wages to her, where she kept them, she told me, safe in her room. When they reached a certain sum, she said, she would give them to my uncle, that he might invest them properly for me. And though I wondered if it was wise to turn my earnings over to anyone, even Mrs. Hastings, I knew no better plan, except to go to Uncle each week with my meager earnings, and I did not care to trouble him with that.

We were nearing the cemetery now, and the

horse seemed surprised when Zeke pulled on the reins, turning him into the entrance and along the winding road among the tombstones. The horse tossed its head and whinnied softly, but Zeke said, "It's okay, Dusty. A quick trip and we'll be on our way again."

I wondered that Zeke should know just where Jade Green was buried, and at first he could not find it, mistaking one gentle slope of green for another. But at last he said, "There it is. I remember now. She was placed near the oak tree, and there's her tombstone."

He pulled the horse and wagon to the side of the road, and I sat for a minute, unsure of going near to the grave. But at last, regaining my courage, I let myself down, Zeke by my side, and slowly walked over to where weeds were already overtaking the headstone. It read thus:

JADE GREEN
APRIL 7, 1869–FEBRUARY 22, 1884
So Short A Stay
Upon This Land
We Grieve Her Death
By Her Own Hand.

I wanted to take a closer look, and as I knelt, brushing away the ivy that was twisting itself around the stone, I saw that someone or something had made a scratch across the last line of the verse.

Fifteen

IN THE days that followed, I left traps all over my uncle's house. Behind the furniture, beneath the draperies, under the beds. Every few days I would change them around, always placing at least one in the root cellar, yet I never caught the hand, and I began to realize just how foolish I was. A hand clever enough to hold a cleaver, a hand talented enough to play the piano, would not be stupid enough to finger its way into a rattrap.

In two weeks' time, I told Mrs. Hastings that although I had caught no rats, they seemed to have been driven from the house, for I saw no more sign

PHYLLIS REYNOLDS NAYLOR

of their presence. She of course was much relieved. If
only the hand could disappear so readily, I thought.

In contrast to the turmoil in my own heart, Uncle
Geoffrey had begun to smile more and more, and
sometimes would even come home of an afternoon
whistling softly to himself. His countenance at the
dinner table was much more pleasant and cheerful
than it had been before, and no sooner would he sit
down than he began to plan how we should spend
the evening.

"I am thinking," he said one night, "that we
should all stroll down to the sea after dinner, Mrs.
Hastings. You must put on your sturdiest shoes, and
Judith can bring the wine flask in a basket. We will sit
on a bench and cool ourselves, watching the sunset."

"You can count me out, Father," Charles replied.
"If I am to go to the seashore I will ride as is my cus-
tom. I'm not a common laborer who hasn't even a
horse to his name."

"Horse or no horse, it is a fit night for walking,"
said my uncle. So we went without my cousin and
had a fine time.

Sometimes, as we enjoyed our salads first in the
garden, Uncle Geoffrey would propose that I play the
piano that night—all songs to be chosen by Mrs.
Hastings. On another night, he might suggest that all

songs would be chosen by him. Or we would play checkers on the large front porch until darkness drove us inside, and then we would light the gas lamps and continue our game.

Some evenings we would all three stroll in the garden, and once I engaged my uncle in a game of hide-and-seek among the hedgerows. So amused was Mrs. Hastings at the sight of my uncle ducking and bobbing around the maze, exclaiming when he saw me, or when I caught him, that she collapsed on a bench with laughter, and we soon joined her, all but winded.

One evening, as we were coming in from the garden, my uncle put one arm around my shoulder, the other around our cook, and said, "I have not been so happy in a long, long time. Judith, you have made this house a lively place indeed, and you, Mrs. Hastings, have kept this house a home. I shall not forget you, I promise."

Mrs. Hastings clucked her tongue, and I in turn did my best to convince him that the pleasure was ours, and that we enjoyed ourselves as much as he. But again he said, "I won't forget you," so I asked if he was going away.

And then he laughed. "No, my dear, but when it comes time for me to leave this earth, you and Mrs.

Hastings will be well provided for, I assure you."

We told him then that we would not listen further to such talk, that the thought of the Sparrow house without him would be too dreadful to contemplate, and so it was, for I knew that with my uncle gone, Charles would move back in overnight, to live as he pleased.

The happier we seemed, however, the more silent Charles became. He would sit at the table saying nothing, perhaps, except to call for the wine or remark on the sauce. I avoided his glance as much as possible, for there was never any charity in his eyes where I was concerned, and scarcely more for Mrs. Hastings. When he did give me his attention, he studied those parts of a woman's body that she takes great pains to conceal, and this made me most uncomfortable indeed.

He usually arrived late, so that he had only to slide in at the table and begin to eat, and left early, taking no part in our checker games or singing once the meal was over. In truth, we were never sorry to see him go, and the subject of Cousin Charles was one Uncle Geoffrey preferred not to bring up. And so we would pass the evening with no mention of him whatever.

I felt I could learn to live this way and be reasonably content—seeing Cousin Charles only at breakfast occasionally, and in the evenings just long enough for dinner. He was now working half days keeping the books for a dentist in Whispers, and in the afternoons, it was said, he went to the racetrack, where he gambled away all he had earned each morning.

Zeke continued to call for me from time to time at the hat shop, and would take me home the long way round through the park. If it were not for Zeke and our rides, and our occasional trips to the cove, I should have been thoroughly miserable, for I did not enjoy the hot, sultry air in Whispers. Perspiration gathered between my breasts and trickled down my back, a most unpleasant sensation, and the bodice of my dress was often soaked through, requiring frequent washings.

But Mrs. Hastings was pleasant and my uncle was kind, and I enjoyed my work at the hat shop, where Violet always supplied me with the latest gossip.

"They say your cousin was drunk on the town last night," she whispered to me one morning. "I hear he was standing outside the Bib and Bottle cursing because they would sell him no more ale." And then she added, "It's not your fault, Love, and I shouldn't have mentioned it. Your uncle is one of the finest men in Whispers, and it's a pity he should have such a son."

"Every family has their problems," I said to Violet,

"and Charles is ours." But within my heart, may God forgive me, I found myself wishing that a carriage might run him over some night in his drunken state, or that he might fall and break his neck. I sucked in my breath, shamed at such a thought, but I could not deny it to myself.

Yet it was far more than Charles that troubled me, and I knew if only I could rid the house of Jade Green, I should be far happier here in Whispers. The ghostly hand could not be caught, and I could not guess its design or purpose. Still, I had not seen it for some weeks, and began to hope that on the days we had kept the door open, the hand might somehow have found its way outside and perhaps gone back to the grave.

One evening, however, after an elderly resident of Whispers had died, Uncle Geoffrey and Mrs. Hastings left to attend the wake. The purpose of their departure made our own house gloomier still, and I busied myself as best I could. I was alone in the parlor, sewing on a button that had come off my shift, when I suddenly heard the piano playing again.

My fingers paused over my sewing, and my heart began to race. Inch by inch I raised my head until the piano was in my sight. There was the hand, practicing upon the keys.

Too roo de nay, too roo de noo . . .

I could not stand the torment.

"No!" I cried, dropping the sewing to my feet and lurching out of my chair.

The hand stopped playing and turned toward me.

"Get out!" I screamed. "Get out of this house! You don't belong here! Go!"

As I moved slowly around the room, the hand pivoted on the keys, as if watching my every step.

I looked for something to grasp, and edged toward the front door, which was propped open with a brick to let in the evening breeze. Without taking my eyes off the hand, I slowly knelt and picked up the doorstop. And then, when the hand stopped playing and began crawling down the leg of the piano, the fingers grasping the wood like some jungle animal scaling a tree, I hurled the brick, striking the ghostly hand a hard blow, one end of the brick gouging the piano leg.

"May that be the end of you!" I cried as the hand dropped to the floor.

But my eyes grew wider still as the hand, quite flat now and lifeless at first, began to move. First the thumb and index finger pulled themselves up and, raising the palm along with them, began the slow crawl across the floor. The smallest finger, however, the pinkie, had been almost severed by the brick, and now dragged motionless behind the others. While I watched in horror, the hand limped its way toward the kitchen. There it stopped and turned stiffly in my direction, as though gazing at me sternly, and then moved more swiftly on into the shadows.

Sixteen

I WAS SICK with terror. Now I had not only the anger of my cousin Charles to contend with, but the wrath of the ghostly fingers as well.

Rushing to my room, I slammed the door behind me, knowing full well that no door, no lock, could keep out Jade Green. I had acted in haste with little thought as to the consequences, and now my life here in Whispers would be the worse for it. What was I to do?

There would be no sleep for me that night, nor would I dare blow out my candle. I went downstairs when I heard Uncle Geoffrey come back with Mrs. Hastings, and told them I would retire early. Mrs.

Hastings, however, was staring at the piano leg.

"What is this?" she asked, bending down to run her hand over the mark I had made.

"I . . . I threw the doorstop," I said. "I'm terribly sorry. The door was open, and a rat ran in and crossed the parlor. I'm afraid I lost my head, and thought to kill it, but only did the piano harm."

It was impossible to know whether she believed me or not, the story itself was so feeble. Indeed, my face burned to tell the lie.

"Well," she said unhappily, "you'd best go to bed. Perhaps I can cover the mark with polish."

I did as she suggested, but did not close my eyes. I propped myself up against my pillows and scanned the room.

Every *creak* of a floorboard, every sigh of the wind, every *click* or *scratch* or *clink*—a branch scraping against my window, even—produced in me such panic that I felt if I were not already mad, I should be so soon. When morning came, I could scarcely move from my bed.

I wanted no questions, however, so I put on my brightest dress, my cheeriest smile, and arrived at the breakfast table as amiable as I could be, concentrating on my tea and biscuit, and ignoring Charles, who always seemed to know when I was upset.

"So, Orphan, is that a false smile I see pasted on your lips this morning or a real one?" he asked.

"One should accept that a smile is a smile and not try to make it other than it is," I told him, continuing the charade even then.

"But are those dark circles I see under your eyes?" he asked. "You did not sleep so well, I take it?"

Had he anything to do with the hand? I wondered. Were they united for my own destruction?

"I am quite well, I assure you," said I, not answering his question directly. And then, to Mrs. Hastings, I added, "I think I shall take my tea in the garden, if you don't mind."

"Of course," she said, "for the air feels as though it will bring rain tomorrow. Enjoy it while you can."

I carried my tea to the table outdoors, but was dismayed when my cousin followed and sat down across from me so that it was most difficult to tip my cup without looking into his eyes.

"So what has waggle-tongue Violet to say about me these days, I wonder?" he began. "Helene too."

"Why not ask them?" said I.

"Because their stories are written all over your face, and I amuse myself reading between the lines." He smiled the sort of smile I did not care for.

"I daresay you already know what is being said

about you," I countered. "You need only look to your own conduct, Charles, for the answer."

"My own conduct?" He laughed heartily. "That I am a man who enjoys his ale? Who appreciates women? Who is challenged by a good bet or a fast horse? Is not such a person a man in every sense, and would you like me less of one?"

"A man, sir, in my opinion, is moderate in his drink, selective in his women, and does not risk his money over a gaming table," I told him.

"Ah! Then you would best stick with your poor Zeke Carey, with his simple pleasures; you'll grow up to marry the simple man, and become a dull wife with simple children."

"My affairs are no concern of yours," I said curtly.

"Or mine yours, then!" he said more jovially. "So let us have no more judgmental scowls from you, Judith. What I do on my own is strictly my business, don't you agree?"

There was truth in what he spoke, and I thought perhaps if I should change my manner toward him, he in turn might behave differently with me. And so, with a deep breath, I extended my hand across the table and said, "Yes, Cousin, I agree. From now on I shall withhold my scowls, if indeed there be any on my face, and shall not meddle in your concerns if you will not meddle in mine."

"Agreed!" said he. "As long as you will allow me to inquire of your health now and then, and to offer my assistance should you need me in any way."

"That would be most charitable of you," I told him, but as I tried to withdraw my hand, he would not allow it and, holding fast to my wrist, ran one finger lightly across my palm, up my arm, leering at me as he attempted to gain entrance into the sleeve of my dress. I jerked myself away from him with such force that I upset my teacup. Charles only laughed as I ran back into the house.

All day the episode weighed on my mind, but Violet was chattering on about a new beau of hers, how they had sneaked off to the shore in the moonlight and gone for a nighttime swim.

My eyes opened wide as I listened to this, and I laughed along with her at her impulsiveness. "But how are your clothes to be dried if there is no sun?" I asked. "How do you explain to your mother when you return that your dress is drenched in salt water?"

This time Violet's eyes fairly danced, and she leaned over so far that her lips touched my ear. "We didn't wear clothes," she told me. "We swam buck naked."

I gasped, my face reddening at the shocking news, but I could not help laughing as well.

"Violet!" said I, glancing around lest we be over-heard. "Surely not!"

She nodded and went on with her stitching, smil-ing still.

"But . . . but, how can you avoid touching each other when you are there in the water together with the waves rolling in?"

And again she leaned my way. "We don't avoid it at all," she said.

I immediately bent over my work, my face red with this new knowledge, trying to imagine Zeke and me on equally familiar terms. I imagined it all too well and felt feverish the rest of the day.

To be young was a most wonderfully scary thing, I decided, for none could know what lay ahead, and there was much to experience. The very same thought brought with it the memory of Jade Green's picture, the way it had appeared for a moment in my mother's frame—so full of life and adventure. She had been rescued from the gutter and placed in my uncle's house, given, I would guess, every opportunity to make something of herself. How could she cut short so young a life? I wondered again as I had so many times before.

"Violet," I found a chance to whisper that after-noon. "How did they know Jade took her own life?

How did they know she wasn't murdered?"

"'Twas plain as day," Violet replied, "and obvious to all she had planned it. For it was wintertime when it happened, and Jade had put on a heavy sweater and hidden herself in the attic. She was found dead on the stairs from loss of blood, her severed hand beside her, and in her other hand, the cleaver."

I closed my eyes and swallowed, remembering the *chop, chop* of the cleaver in the kitchen, and later, the sight of the partially severed finger trailing after the others. All afternoon I thought of Jade Green's death, and it was still on my mind when I rode home in the wagon with Zeke.

When I mentioned it to him, however, he said, "It's a strange way to die, I'll grant you, but do you have to dwell so much on this, Judith? Can't you add a little fun to your life?"

He was right, of course.

"What would you have me do?" I asked defensively. And then, on impulse, I added, "Swim in the sea buck naked?" My cheeks suddenly turned bright red, that I should say such words to him aloud.

He turned to me in such surprise that I laughed to see his face. Zeke chuckled all the way home, and was smiling yet when I jumped off the wagon and ran inside.

At dinner that evening, Uncle Geoffrey seemed of an unusually serious nature, and just before Mrs. Hastings brought out the cake and berries, he said, "Charles, if you have no urgent business after dinner, I would like you to stay for a time, as I have something to discuss while we are all at the table."

"Does it concern me alone, Father, and is an audience required?" Charles asked.

"It concerns all in this room," said Uncle Geoffrey. "So if you would be so good, sir, as to stay a short while . . ."

I wished he had announced this after the cake had been served, for I was so worried as to what he might say that I scarce enjoyed my dessert.

When the cake had been eaten, the tea brought for the ladies and brandy for the men, Uncle Geoffrey leaned back in his chair, one hand in his vest pocket, and said: "I am leaving town for two days and will be in Charleston on business; it's time I went over my financial holdings, updated my will, and saw to other matters.

"What I would like to state, however, in the presence of all three of you, is that I am directing my attorney, in the event of my death, to divide my property thus: The house shall go to you, Mrs. Hastings, who has cared for it so faithfully all these years, with the condition that Judith be allowed to remain here and call it home for as long as she likes." Charles gasped, but his father continued, "All the rest of my holdings—my land, my accounts, my stocks and bonds—shall be divided three ways: one-tenth to you, Mrs. Hastings, and the other ninety percent to be divided equally between Judith and Charles."

A chair scraped as Charles rose to his feet, his face contorted with rage. The sight of him frightened me greatly. Mrs. Hastings, in fact, was as pale as flour.

"This is an outrage, Father, and an insult to your rightful heir," said he and, turning so suddenly that his chair tipped over backward and crashed to the floor, he strode out of the room and left the house.

Seventeen

I DISCOVERED THAT I was to be provided for the rest of my life, and that I had made a mortal enemy, all in a space of minutes. My uncle's announcement had brought such joy and relief to both Mrs. Hastings and me that all we had been able to was repeat, "Oh, sir!" and "Oh, Uncle!" again and again. But with the sudden and angry departure of my cousin, we quickly fell silent and stared after him, not knowing what to do.

"Don't worry about Charles," said Uncle Geoffrey. "He will have quite enough money to sustain him the rest of his life, even if he doesn't deserve it. But I will rest easier knowing that the two of you are provided for also."

"You are most generous and kind!" insisted Mrs. Hastings, and I said also that this was far more than I ever expected of him.

But Uncle just clapped his hands and said we would talk no more about it. He would like another piece of Mrs. Hastings' cake, and then he should like nothing so much as for the three of us to walk down to the shore again and sit awhile, for autumn was coming soon and there would not be many of these warm evenings left. And so we set out, the three of us, and enjoyed the ocean breeze playing on our faces as we watched the waves swell and break.

A group of young men came by, one of them Zeke, riding their unicycles on the boardwalk, and when Zeke saw me, he went through a wondrous performance of turns and spins, backing up and pivoting, so that we began to applaud. At that the other five men came back, and they rode in a line in front of us, as if onstage. My uncle laughed so, it was worth the walk down from the house just to see him enjoying himself.

"Zeke Carey, you watch out or a circus will have you!" Mrs. Hastings cried. "You're better at your unicycle than you are with your father's horse and wagon, I'll wager."

"Now, Mrs. Hastings, no one has complained yet about my service," Zeke told her. "And if you make a complaint, I swear I will run off to the circus and take Judith with me."

At that, Uncle Geoffrey and Mrs. Hastings laughed again. I liked hearing Zeke talk so in front of the other lads. All the same, my cheeks blushed, but Zeke threw me a kiss as he pedaled away. I remembered the first time we had gone to the cove, and the way his lips had kissed mine as we folded the blanket.

The following day Uncle Geoffrey packed his valise as I prepared to set out for Helene's Hat Shoppe. Charles did not come for breakfast that morning. In fact, I wondered if we should see him ever again, he was so angry when he left the table the previous night.

"Good-bye, Uncle," I said. "We shall see you in two days' time then. Have a safe journey."

The sky did not please me as I made my way toward town. The clouds had an unfriendly look, reminding me of the day I had first come to Whispers, but I told myself that the weather cannot always be fair—in Ohio as well as the Carolinas—and so I worked cheerfully in the hat shop, putting a new display of fall bonnets in the window for ladies to admire.

At lunchtime, I traded secrets with Violet. When I told her about Zeke saying that he would run off with me to the circus, she said, "Mrs. Hastings had better watch out that he doesn't run off with you to marry. For I've seen the fond way he looks at you when he's waiting outside in the wagon."

"Oh, nonsense!" I told her, but in my heart I knew it was true.

When I arrived home that afternoon, Uncle Geoffrey had gone, and Mrs. Hastings was hard at work in the root cellar, making room for the potatoes and onions and turnips we should store when the weather grew colder. I did not mind work in the root cellar, for it was the coolest place to be on a warm day, and I liked the dank smell of earth; liked walking about on the straw and counting the apples and potatoes still left in the bins.

Mrs. Hastings had started up the short flight of stairs to the kitchen above with an apron full of potatoes, and I was close behind her, when suddenly she gave a scream and dropped her apron. Potatoes rained down on me, and I put out my arms in case she should fall.

"Mrs. Hastings, what is it?" I cried, stumbling up the steps beside her.

But the poor woman could not speak—her face was as white as milk. She grabbed hold of my arm and screamed again, pointing, and there, coming across the kitchen floor, was the ghostly hand, dragging its half-severed finger like a tail.

I reached forward, gripping the door handle, and pulled the door shut with a *bang,* which was useless, of course, for the hand could easily have flattened itself on its palm and edged under. But I knew not what else to do to calm the cook down, afraid her heart might give way.

I helped her down the steps and onto the old cobbler's bench, where we often sat when we sorted apples. Her eyes were as large as coat buttons, however, and words wouldn't come. She only clutched at my arm, trembling.

Finally she said, "It's her, then. The ghost of Jade Green."

"You've seen it before?" I asked. "The hand?"

"Mercy, child, no! But what else could it be? Oh, after her death, we heard such shrieks and moans from that room where she died, it was enough to break one's heart and chill the bones, I tell you. But once we rid the house of all she held dear, the sounds came no more, and we were sure we were quit of her."

There came a scurrying, scratching sound from the door of the root cellar, and again Mrs. Hastings gave a cry and cowered against the wall, hands over her face.

In the flickering glow of the candle, I watched for the first sign of those thin, white fingers, working themselves through the crack under the door, but they did not appear. Instead, it sounded as though the hand were climbing up the wall and door frame. And then . . . a noise that stopped my breath: the metallic *click* of the bolt, locking the door from outside.

Eighteen

G OD HELP us!" cried Mrs. Hastings in despair, and I began to think we were done for at last, trapped like two rats in a hole. I now began to shiver so violently that the dear woman forgot her own apprehensions and proceeded to comfort me.

"Someone will find us," she said. "Someone will come, and if we have to spend two days here before your uncle returns, well . . . we will be miserable, I warrant, but we shan't die."

My trembling did not subside, however, for in truth it was born not so much of fear as of guilt. The small flame of the melting candle struggled to keep its glow amid the hot wax, and finally turned blue and died, leaving us both in darkness, and I knew that if I were ever to tell my guilty secret, it must be now.

"Mrs. Hastings," I wept, "I need to ask your forgiveness. Yours and my uncle's too."

"Why, child, whatever for? What could you possibly have done that would make you talk so?"

As I continued to weep, she put her arms around me and rocked me like a babe, my tears moistening the front of her shift.

"It's all my fault," I sobbed. "The hand . . . the ghost . . . everything that's happened lately is because of me."

Slowly she stopped rocking but held me still. I felt her great chest expand as she took a breath, and finally she said, "You brought something green into this house. . . ."

"Yes," I said, pulling away from her then, and, in the refuge of darkness, confessed what I had done.

"I did not think that my mother's picture, in the green silk frame, could do anyone harm," I finished, beginning to cry all over again. "I had vowed never to take it out of the trunk where my uncle might see it and be upset."

Once again I felt the good woman sigh as she patted my back. "I think I knew we could not keep Jade

Green away forever," she said. "At some time or other, someone would bring the color into the house again, or we would find something left behind by that poor child. I wish you had obeyed your uncle's instructions, though; how much simpler things would have been. But I don't know, had I been in your place, that I could have left behind a picture frame given me by my mother either. So we will have to deal with it the best we can."

It was at that moment we heard footsteps. Why we both did not cry out at once, I don't know. But they were not the footsteps of my uncle, and, indeed, sounded so strange, so secretive, that we both stopped breathing and lifted our heads to listen.

The sound came from the back porch, hesitant soft footsteps, and then the creak of the door as it opened.

All was silence, and Mrs. Hastings was about to call out when I clutched at her arm, yet I knew not why.

There were three more footsteps, a pause, three more . . .

"They're out, then?" we heard Charles murmur. "So much the better for me."

Mrs. Hastings sharply drew in her breath.

The soft footsteps continued, a few at a time, like

a man cautiously making his way about. Then the creak of the stairs to the second floor.

I had visions of the hand following along beside him on the banister, pointing him back down again, beckoning toward the door of the root cellar, where we were trapped.

In a while, though, all noise stopped. We didn't know if Charles was upstairs or down, still in the house or gone. Mrs. Hastings began to cry silently in fright.

"He's up to no good, you can bet," she wept.

"Shhhh," I whispered in her ear. "We have to be quiet. If he sees that the door to the root cellar is locked, he won't guess we're here."

It was perhaps twenty minutes before we heard Charles's footsteps on the stairs again. He seemed to be making a slow tour of the downstairs rooms. We could hear doors opening, checking to see if we were in Uncle's study, out in the sunroom, the parlor. . . . The footsteps came back to the kitchen again and stopped just outside the cellar door.

"Out for a walk, are they?" he murmured. "Well, when they come back, they're in for a surprise. . . ." We heard the back door open, and a minute later his carriage rolled away.

Had the hand somehow known he was coming?

I wondered. Had the ghost of Jade Green purposely locked us in here so that Charles would not guess we were down in the cellar? Was it possible that the hand was no enemy after all, just the sad ghost of a girl whose life had become so unbearable that she decided to end it?

But just as Mrs. Hastings and I began to sigh with relief that Charles was gone, the sigh turned into a gasp and the gasp became a sharp cry.

For both of us, at the same time, smelled smoke.

Ninenteen

I SCREAMED, BUT Mrs. Hastings had begun to pray. She broke off in the middle of the prayer and began to cry, her voice shaky and high.

"There's no window, child, to crawl out of, no water to wet down our clothes. If the smoke doesn't get us, the floor above us will burn and come crashing down on our heads! Oh, mercy!"

The smoke grew stronger still, and was soon accompanied by a crackling sound. Together we screamed and called, and it was only a minute before Mrs. Hastings passed out and crumpled to the floor, not from the smoke but from terror.

At that very moment I heard yells from outside—then still more shouts. Running feet, footsteps pounding on the porch, the old gardener's excited voice, and then Zeke calling: "Judith! Judith!"

"Here!" I screamed. "In the root cellar! Oh, hurry!"

There was the *clink* once more of the metal lock, a burst of daylight, the smoke-filled kitchen, flames, and the next I knew I was drenched by buckets of water being thrown at the fire by the neighbors. Mrs. Hastings was carried through the burning kitchen to the grass outside, and I followed close behind.

"It's out, now," a man called.

"Was a kitchen fire, then," called another.

"You've a blackened wall and ceiling, Miss, but beyond that, it's not much harm done," said a third.

The neighbor women were reviving poor Mrs. Hastings, and when she opened her eyes to see the damange the fire had done, she swooned again. But within the hour, the neighbors were scrubbing down the soot and carting out burned plaster.

"How did it happen?" they asked.

"What were you cooking?"

"Where were the men?"

"It's all a muddle," I told them.

Everyone went away finally but Zeke, and I knew

there would be no escaping his questions, for it was he who had unlocked the cellar door.

I made a broth and some buttered toast for Mrs. Hastings and took her up to bed, with Zeke's promise that he would stay watch the whole night. It was only when I was fetching her nightdress for her that we discovered her dresser had been searched, the drawers opened, the contents scattered. Only then did we find that her most recent savings were gone, and mine along with them.

"Oh, child!" she exclaimed. "It is Charles's doing as sure as I breathe." She wept a little then, but when we compared the loss of our earnings to the saving of our lives, we could not help but feel fortunate.

After I had closed her door and gone downstairs again, I went into the parlor and sat on the sofa with Zeke, telling him of the money that was missing.

"Judith," he said, "there is something more you're not telling me. Who locked you in the root cellar? Was it Charles?"

"It was Charles, perhaps, who set the fire, but he did not lock the door," I said.

"Who was it, then?"

"That I can't tell you, Zeke, for you would never believe me, and I should be shut away as a mad-woman. The answer must stay with me."

Very gently he took my hand. "If the answer stays with you, then it comes between us. You *must* tell me. Was it your uncle?"

"Uncle Geoffrey? Never. He has gone to Charleston."

"And it wasn't Charles. The gardener?"

"No, not he."

"Then who is left?"

"I dare not say."

Zeke looked straight into my eyes. "I give you my solemn word that you shall not be locked up, no matter how much I disbelieve you."

"But it's a strange story, Zeke."

"Then begin," said he, and put one arm about my shoulder.

And so, snuggled as I was against him, beneath his protective arm, I began the tale—my mother's picture, the green silk frame, the scratching, gnawing sound in the closet, and the hand . . . the ghostly hand . . . at the piano, holding the cleaver, the severed finger. . . .

"You're imagining things! You must be!" Zeke insisted.

And just as firmly I declared I was not—that I could scarce believe it myself.

When I had finished, there was a silence so long, I feared that my story had put him to sleep. When I looked in his eyes, however, I saw his concern.

"At least you are safe," he said.

"But you don't believe me."

"I believe you think you saw what you said."

"Yet you truly believe I did not see it at all!" I retorted.

"It's too bizarre to be believed!"

"Am I mad, then?"

"No. Confused, perhaps."

"But we were locked in the root cellar, Zeke. You saw it yourself. Clearly we did not lock ourselves in."

"Perhaps Charles is the one who did it," he said. And then, taking my hands, he said, "I'll tell no one, Judith, for I truly don't care. Mad or not, you are the one I love."

He took me in his arms and I lay against his chest, his ribs against my ribs, his chest against my bosom, our lips exchanging the sweetest taste, the lightest touch, the most ardent protestations of love, so that my entire body tingled and warmed to the thought of lying abed with him.

But as I turned to kiss the side of his neck, I saw a slight movement across the room, and looked up to see the hand of Jade Green walking across the top of the piano.

I gasped and pointed. Zeke Carey sat up and stared.

The hand walked along the rim of the music holder and down onto the keys. And then, the pinkie dragging still, they began their slow dance:

Too roo de nay, too roo de noo,
Too roo de nay, too roo de noo . . .

Twenty

WHEN UNCLE Geoffrey returned, he declared that Charles would no longer be welcome in the house. Indeed, until he apologized and set things right, he should not be admitted at all. Having divided the property in his will into three portions, my uncle said, he was prepared to go back to Charleston if necessary and divide it into two portions only.

But such talk only made Mrs. Hastings and me all the more anxious, and we had worries enough as it was. If Charles was cut out of the will entirely, what might he not do? The question I could not answer in my heart was who had set the fire. Had Jade Green locked us in the root cellar to protect us from Charles or to make us the victims of a fire? If the gardener had not detected the flames, and Zeke unlocked the door, would the hand have returned to let us out? The cook and I had already agreed between us that we would not tell my uncle about the hand and upset him further. So one moment I worried about the hand, the next I found myself lost in a daydream of Zeke and his warm embrace, and the next I worried about Charles's return, whether he would come again in the night; be waiting for me behind a closed door.

Rumor went about that it was he who had locked us in the root cellar and set the house afire, which did much harm to his already damaged reputation. Helene even reported that he had drunkenly tried to embrace her one afternoon when she passed him on the street.

It broke my heart to see the pain this caused my uncle, but when he spoke of going to Charleston to remove Charles's name from his will entirely, I dissuaded him, reminding him that many a prodigal son has returned home all the better for his experience.

And so, after the workmen had come and gone, and the kitchen of the Sparrow house was in order once more, the three of us—Uncle, Mrs. Hastings, and myself—tried to settle down to an ordinary life; as ordinary as a life can be with Jade Green about. Autumn was upon us, and days were spent at the hat shop helping women select their fall bonnets; evenings found me playing the piano for my uncle, engaging in a game of checkers, or reading aloud to Mrs. Hastings as she did her embroidery work in the parlor. And when I could, I met Zeke at the back of the garden, or we kissed in the wagon riding home. He was quiet as to the hand, however; more solemn than I had ever seen him.

"I can't explain it," he said to me, "but I know what we saw. You didn't imagine it, Judith. I was mistaken."

Mrs. Hastings, however, was clearly upset. I knew what she was thinking when the breeze suddenly blew a curtain, or a paper slid from a chair across the floor. Any slight movement anywhere in the room made her turn quickly, and I noticed she was most careful where she put her feet. We kept our fears from Uncle Geoffrey, however, for he had Charles on his mind, and that was enough.

A fortnight after the fire, my uncle stood at the window after dinner, gazing upward at the sky. "It's hurricane weather," he told me, "and the fishermen say it's a hurricane sky."

I had never been through a hurricane, of course,

and found such talk full of adventure, but Mrs. Hastings did not share my excitement. "I have lived through several in my time, and would not like to go through one again," she said.

There was much talk in town of the coming storm, if indeed the fishermen were right, but it seemed so distant. The women of Whispers, in fact, were thinking ahead to Christmas, ordering their holiday bonnets. I frequently went to the window of the hat shop, however, and glanced at the sky.

"Oh, I wouldn't pay it much mind," said Violet, trying on a brown and yellow hat she had just made for a grand lady in Savannah, who would have none other than Helene's Hat Shoppe make all her fine bonnets and send them down by carriage. "There's always talk, talk, talk during hurricane season, but one rarely strikes at us."

Riding home in Zeke's wagon as he made his deliveries, I listened to him tell how the sea turned up in a storm, waves eighteen feet high. "It's the land farther up that gets it most," he said. "Especially Cape Hatteras in North Carolina, which stretches out into the sea."

But I wasn't thinking of the sea just then, I was thinking of Zeke's back, his shoulders two round swells that rippled and rolled beneath his shirt, and I thought if I could but have Zeke to protect me always, what harm could possibly befall me?

It was at night when the fears unloosed themselves and roamed about within my mind. For as long as Charles was without the house, plotting against those who were within, and the hand, the ghostly hand, was hiding who knew where, how could I think of future happiness?

There were even times, God forgive me, in the darkest night when my wakefulness unleashed every fear within the human heart, and I trusted no one. Was it not possible, my mad mind would venture, that my uncle had not gone to Charleston at all, but was himself responsible for the hand, just to frighten me and drive me to the same fate my mother had suffered? Or that Mrs. Hastings and Charles were in a plot together, and although it appeared he had stolen our earnings, hers and mine, in truth they had merely made it appear so, and would split my portion between them? Even Zeke, at times, seemed suspect. What if, in spite of all his protestations, he were responsible for the hand, and after Mrs. Hastings and I had returned to the root cellar, it was he himself who had locked the door?

Of course, none of this made much sense, for why would my uncle or Mrs. Hastings or Zeke wish me harm? And then I would be rocked by the worst fear of all, that everything I thought had happened had, in truth, not happened at all, and that only by the kindness of others was this lunatic girl allowed to live in Whispers, protected by her uncle and his cook.

In the mornings, however, with the autumn sun shining through my window, my worries seemed so unreasonable that I faced the day with new confidence, eager to drink my morning tea with Mrs. Hastings, to chatter with Violet at lunchtime, and ride home, if I were lucky, with Zeke.

But this particular Saturday I awoke to such a wind that all the shutters on the Sparrow house rattled and shook.

"It's a blow, all right!" Mrs. Hastings told me. "You won't be going to the hat shop today, my dear. In fact, Helene stopped by to say that all the shops were closed."

Uncle did not go to his place of business, either, but put on his mackintosh and boots and walked down the street to the barbershop where the men had gathered, to determine the course of the storm. It was generally predicted that the hurricane, although close, would largely pass us by.

By two o'clock, however, there was a sudden shift in the wind, and it was evident that the storm was bearing down upon us. Whether the major damage would be here or elsewhere was of little consequence, for what could be seen with the naked eye was frightening enough.

Uncle Geoffrey came back from the barbershop instructing us to close the shutters. He fretted that he had not had special shutters made to cover the stained-glass panels that formed an arch above the parlor windows as well as the door. When Zeke came by to see if help were needed, Uncle sent him off at once to fetch wood planks to secure over the stained glass.

Mrs. Hastings and I were told to pack up the most valuable breakables and Uncle would drive us inland to Mrs. Hastings' brother some distance away. By the time we had loaded them into the carriage along with Mrs. Hastings and her valise, however, there was scarcely room for Uncle, much less for me.

"We will leave some of the valuables behind, Judith," he said. "We'll not go off without you."

"I'll come with Zeke," I told him, wishing it so in any case. "I can help him nail the wood over the windows, Uncle. Do go on and be quick!"

Uncle Geoffrey started to protest, but Zeke cut in: "I will have her on the way within an hour," he said. "My wagon is sturdy, and I know the road to White Hall."

And when my uncle made to unload his carriage further so that I might ride, I said, "Think of your stained-glass windows, Uncle! It takes two to board them up—one to hammer and one to hold the wood steady. There is no one else to help—everyone is taking care that his own house should not float away."

"Promise me you will deliver her safely," my uncle said, grasping Zeke's arm, which was, in truth, more sturdy than his own.

"You have my word," said Zeke.

And so my uncle and Mrs. Hastings departed, the horse splashing through water that was already rushing down the street, and Zeke and I set to work nailing the boards over the yellow and purple glass that adorned each window overlooking the front porch. The wind howled so fiercely, we could scarce hear our own voices, and the rain blew sideways, almost knocking me off my feet.

When we were nailing the last panel, Zeke yelled, "I can finish this myself, Judith. Go pack your bag and be sure that the house is locked up. We must be on our way before the water gets any higher."

Hurrying to my room, I pulled out my smallest valise, and in it I placed my shawl and linens, my stockings and brush. I folded my best gown with the lace around the bottom, secretly dreaming of being unable to reach my uncle, and hence stranded some-where with Zeke for the night, wrapped in his strong arms. The very thought made my pulse race.

There were footsteps on the stairs, and I thought of showing him my nightdress before I packed it, so that he might imagine me in it. In fact, I was holding it to me as I stepped out into the hall, and then I choked back a cry as I saw my cousin advancing toward me, with as lecherous a look as I had ever seen on his face.

With a scream I dashed back into my room, slam-ming the door behind me, but before I could turn the lock, the door burst open and in Charles came.

"Get out!" said I, noting his drunken gait, yet my eyes were riveted on him, for they were not the eyes of a man in a stupor so much as a man driven by lust and rage. Indeed, as I challenged him, he merely laughed and was already, to my horror, unbuttoning his waistcoat.

I flung myself across the bed to reach the other side and, yanking open the drawer of my bedside table, retrieved the knife I had once hidden there.

As I stood, the knife raised, it seemed only to excite him more, and he laughed menacingly as he approached in a half circle, hands out in front of him like a wrestler.

"If you touch me, sir, this knife shall stab you through!" I told him, but his eyes only glowed with the challenge.

"That's what *she* said, only she had a cleaver," he laughed.

"Jade Green?" I gasped, thinking of the poor creature hiding on the attic stairs. But not for a moment did I take my eyes off Charles, or my hand from the knife. With my other hand, I tried to open the window behind me, in hopes of escaping that way if there were no other, but it rose only a little and stopped, the howling wind and the rain rushing in through the opening in the shutters.

"What I asked of her was so little," Charles went on. "The same I asked of you. A kiss. Only you wouldn't give it to me, would you? So I shall take that kiss now, Orphan, and more besides."

"You shall not!" I cried. "Zeke is here! He will come!" I moved farther away from him, but saw I was being backed into a corner between wall and bed, and screamed in terror.

"He'll have to break in first, for I've locked all the doors," said Charles, and with that, he lunged for me, grabbing my wrist and forcing me down onto the bed.

Again I screamed, but he pressed one hand over

my mouth. Desperately I held on to the knife, though my strength was no match for his, and I could not move my arm to strike him.

"Don't be stupid, Orphan," he said, his whiskey breath in my face. "You knife me and I'll do the same to you I did to Jade. You will stab yourself with your own hand, only it will be mine guiding it to your heart."

With that he was upon me, pinning my arms to the bed and forcing the knife from my fingers.

Was it over, then? I wondered. By the time Zeke broke in, would I be ravished, losing not only my honor but possibly my life?

And then I saw it . . . the hand. It was climbing swiftly up the bedpost now and onto my pillow. Charles pressed me down with one knee as he began to unfasten his trousers, then startled suddenly as he glimpsed the hand.

He let out a cry, reeling backward as it leaped from my pillow and grasped his throat. In that same instant I slid from the bed and ran screaming from the room, half tumbling down the stairs.

There was pounding on the front door.

"Judith!" came Zeke's voice. "Judith!"

In shock, I opened it and pulled Zeke inside, speaking incoherently.

He clutched my shoulders. "What's wrong with you? Why did you lock the door? We have to leave at once!"

"Zeke . . . come!" I cried, and as he followed me up the stairs, I told him briefly, in gasps and sobs, what had happened.

In my room, Charles lay dead upon the floor, his shirtwaist out, his trousers unbuttoned, the butcher knife still clasped in his hand. His glassy eyes stared unseeing at the ceiling, but the marks on his neck were already beginning to fade, for the ghostly fingers told no tales. The hand that had come to save me was nowhere in sight.

Zeke and I clung to each other until our shaking subsided. Then he picked up my valise and, with one arm around my shoulder, hurried me down the stairs.

We closed the door behind us, and a torrent of rain hit our faces. Beyond the iron gate, the street had become a river. Dusty, the horse, whinnied, then lowered his head against the gale. We were the last wagon to leave Whispers.

"Hurry!" said Zeke.

As I climbed into the wagon, glancing one last time at the house, a sudden movement caught my eye.

Crawling along the porch roof from the back of the house came the hand. The fingers made their way across the shingles to the drainpipe, and then began their slow descent.

The horse and wagon began to move, and I could feel the warmth of Zeke's leg against mine, but I turned in my seat, my eyes riveted upon the hand. Down it came, lower, then lower still, until it reached the swirling water and disappeared.

Forever.